A CURSE, A KEY, & A CORKSCREW

CHAPTER 1

J oan Sinclair turned the key over in her hand. She turned it over
again, then tossed it into the air. As she reached to catch it, it
awkwardly bounced off the side of her palm and clattered to the
metal lab table in front of her. Yeah, that seemed about right.
She left it where it was, staring at it as she chewed on the tip of
her thumb.

It was a skeleton key — not an ornate object that you could
imagine opening a pirate chest or the perfumed boudoir of a
Victorian courtesan, but a prosaic one, the kind that might open
the dusty drawer of an old desk found in your grandmother's
attic, tucked behind a stuffed owl and a painting of seven
apron-clad carrots performing a ritual sacrifice of a beet.

The key was made of brass with an oval loop at one end, two
jagged teeth at the other, and a short shaft connecting them.
Its only concession to aesthetics was a single decorative groove
down the barrel.

But it had called to Joan.

She had been walking past Shiny Ol' Junk, an antique shop
in the quaint downtown of her small community, enjoying the
first crisp autumn day as the bracing breeze caressed her face,
ruffling her shoulder-length honey-colored hair and blowing the
ends of her knitted purple scarf away from her body. She had
laughed with delight and glanced at her reflection in the window.

And then she had looked through the glass at a wooden bowl of vintage keys next to the register and her gaze had fallen upon one unassuming key sitting partially submerged a little to the right of the center. She had stopped short, her body going rigid, rocked by a familiar electric jolt, just like the one she'd felt that fateful day when she was six years old — twenty-nine years, seven months, and eight days ago.

Her smile had faded, and the chill air felt colder, no longer pleasantly brisk, but a harbinger of winter to come. This key was obviously cursed — as cursed as Joan herself. This might be her chance to undo the jinx before it was too late. She had rushed into the store to purchase the key.

Joan put her head down on the table, the smooth metal cool against her cheek, staring at the fallen key from the side. There was a tiny streak of tarnish just below where the teeth met the barrel, and she found herself transfixed by it, her mind hiking a well-worn path back to that terrible, unforgettable Monday afternoon.

The rain had been continually beating against the classroom windows all morning, so she and her first-grade class had been deprived of their outdoor recess. This was nothing out of the ordinary for March in Oregon, but on this morning, their teacher, Mrs. Olsen, had been suffering from an intense migraine.

Mrs. Olsen's patience had worn thin as the day dragged on and the class grew more and more restless, their piping voices grating her nerves, her pleas for calm ignored. They had returned from pizza day in the cafeteria full of vim and rambunctiousness, squirming in their desks and shouting to each other across the room. Whatever she did, the teacher just couldn't convince them to sit quietly and focus.

Joan was a naturally reserved child and wasn't participating in the rowdiness. She and her best friend, Sadie, had been sitting off to the side, happily coloring and whispering together, making up a story about the fairy tale scene on the pages in front of them, crayons smearing their gritty hues over bunnies, gnomes, trees, and a castle in the distant background.

Then she had caught a whiff of an acrid, burning smell. Glancing up, Joan had stared at Mrs. Olsen's face, at her deep brown eyes uncannily glowing, black smoke curling from her short tawny hair. She had gasped as she watched sparks emanating from those eyes, the smoke growing in volume, hovering in a cloud above the teacher's head.

And then another girl, Beth Fiorella, a high-strung child who was prone to histrionics, had also looked up and begun a shrill banshee-like wail.

At that, Mrs. Olsen's face had fallen into a bizarre blankness, the entirety of her eyes becoming solid black almonds, her visage slackening. She had ponderously stood from her old-fashioned desk, and the class had finally, gradually, quieted at the sight, except for Beth, who continued to scream.

Mrs. Olsen's head had turned like a searchlight, her gaze slow and heavy, her dark stare freezing each child as it passed. When she'd gotten to Beth, the girl's mouth had snapped shut with a final whimper. And Mrs. Olsen had spoken quietly, evenly, into the silence.

"I have your attention right now,
And I'll keep it awhile, I vow.
In one score and ten,
I will see you again.
To silence and darkness you'll bow."

Mrs. Olsen had paused. Then her voice had risen, building a pyramid of sound. "And so I curse you — and I curse you — I curse you — curse you!" Each phrase a higher level, ending with a brief wordless scream to rival Beth's.

As the shriek left her throat, each child in the room felt a stabbing bolt of electricity from head to toe, just like the one Joan was to experience years later, upon catching sight of the skeleton key.

Beth and two others had fainted dead away and a few more had wet themselves. All of the class found themselves unable to speak at all or with diminished voices and most found themselves blind as well. Joan herself had lost her voice for the rest of the day, her throat dry and her vision fracturing like an old deteriorated film.

The teacher had taken in a deep breath and then sat down with a *THUNK*. All around the room, frightened children sat in silence, too terrified to move.

Through a haze, Joan saw Mrs. Olsen's body sway and collapse, her head falling onto her desk. She fell into a deep sleep, snores drifting through the otherwise silent room, as the class desperately struggled to make any sound.

The children trembled in their desks. Those who had been away from their seats groped and stumbled into any empty ones they could find. They sat, numb and dazed, for what felt like hours. Joan later learned it had only been a few minutes before another teacher came in to investigate the shouting.

He had entered the room, found it full of traumatized students and a sleeping teacher, and taken immediate action. Other adults were brought in. The school nurse took one look and insisted on calling in a doctor. Those who had had accidents were cleaned up and the fainted revived. Parents were called and most took their progeny straight to the hospital, where the staff were stumped.

Many unsuccessful attempts were made to wake up Mrs. Olsen and finally an ambulance was summoned to take her away. She had remained in a coma for about a year and then disappeared from her long-term care facility. As the kids got older, some of them had tried to find her to demand answers, but there was no trace.

Over the course of the next few days, everyone gradually regained their sight and voices and were released from the hospital and cleared to return to school. The principal assigned the class a substitute teacher and a therapist, who asked gentle questions and administered extensive psychiatric tests. She never did figure out what had happened, dismissing their tales of a curse and a teacher on fire as a mass hallucination.

Most of the students eventually lost interest, their trauma fading as time passed. But a few, Joan included, just couldn't get past it. Through the years, even as some transferred to other schools, even past graduation, even though they didn't always get along, they kept in touch. These few class members became obsessed with the curse, devoting their lives to lifting it, finding careers in curse-related fields or jobs that required little time and energy, allowing them to focus on research and experiments.

And as time went on, the urgency grew. "One score and ten" was thirty years. What would happen in thirty years?

Chapter 2

As she lifted her head and picked up the key again, running her fingers over it, memorizing the smoothness of the shaft and the ins and outs of the teeth, Joan knew she needed to tell the others. Their thirty-year timeline had diminished to five months, and this was their first real lead. She was in over her head.

But first — wine.

She left her physics lab, striding through her backyard and into the kitchen, and pulled a bottle of red wine from the rack on the countertop. She rummaged in a drawer for a corkscrew. Her fingers found one right away, but it was that crappy one that Brandon had left behind once after a disastrous picnic situation.

It was the kind of corkscrew where you stab the cork and then twist it in, and then you push down the wings on the sides, and *supposedly*, they would move the cork up and out, but really it usually moves it about a centimeter and then you have to wiggle and wiggle and wiggle it for a zillion years until half of it comes out in your hand and the other half falls into the wine. Joan was in no kind of mental state to deal with that bullshit.

She opened up the drawer all the way, peering into its deepest corners, searching for her preferred corkscrew, the one that looked like a Swiss Army knife, where you just twisted it into the cork and then levered the side doohickey, little by little, up the bottleneck. That one always worked. Plus it had a nifty little blade for cutting the foil and a tab that you could use to make citrus twists for your cocktails. Joan wasn't ruling out the possibility that she would be moving on to cocktails later.

She pulled the drawer out entirely, setting it on the counter and shoving aside a cacophony of chopsticks and spatulas, a potato masher and a vegetable peeler, nested spoons and measuring cups. She poked herself on a corn-on-the-cob holder she hadn't used in years and snatched her hand back, sucking on the tip of her finger and glowering at the assortment of useless crap.

Her easy-to-use corkscrew was nowhere to be found. Finally, she picked up the other one and gave it a look typically reserved for war criminals and door-to-door missionaries.

"Fine. I'll use this one," she muttered. She sat down at the table, just for a moment, to psych herself up, dropping her head back to stare at the ceiling. There was a smattering of something pinkish up there, to her left. She glanced down at the countertop below it. The spatter was directly above the blender, possibly indicating a smoothie or daiquiri incident. She didn't remember it.

Daiquiri, then. Or maybe Sadie had done it and hadn't told her. Which still argued for a daiquiri.

Actually, maybe a daiquiri sounded better right now than wine. First, though, she'd better clean off the ceiling.

She pushed herself up out of her chair and walked over to the broom closet, pulling out a sponge mop and carrying it to the sink to wet it. As she scrubbed at her ceiling, lukewarm dirty water trickling down the mop handle and hitting her hand, she knew she was putting off the moment when she had to put out the word about the key. Maybe she should call Brandon or Sadie first instead.

She shook her head, sending blonde hair flying into her face. She tipped her head to shake it back. This was the first actual clue to their specific situation, not theoretical studies of magic or energy work or ghost-hunting or neuropsychology or physics, and it needed to be addressed, especially as they neared that thirty-year mark. She couldn't keep it within her small group of friends — they would need the expertise of the whole curse-obsessed gang.

Joan swung the mop down and rinsed it in the sink. She wrung it out, cursing and sputtering as the smelly, gritty water squirted her in the face. She grabbed the hand towel from its hook beside the window and dabbed her face clean, then carried the mop out to the back porch, stopping on her way to snag a bottle of rum from the top of the fridge.

Screw the daiquiri. This was the important part anyway.

She sat down at her patio table, unscrewed the lid from the bottle — so simple! Why had she been messing around with corkscrews and wine bottles, anyway? — then pulled her phone from her jeans pocket, opened her browser, and pulled up the group forum used by those members of the class who still involved themselves in lifting the curse. She took a swig of rum, grimacing as the bittersweet booze hit her tastebuds.

Joan set the bottle on the table and closed her eyes, struggling to gather her thoughts into a tidy queue, but ending up with a stampede. She corralled them into two groups: helpful and panicky. The panicky thoughts mustered into a large, nervous herd, and she sent them galloping off into the distance, focusing in on the small clump of helpful notions.

She opened her eyes and began to type.

I found something today, at an antique shop in town. I don't know where it came from or what it means. It's just a skeleton key, but it called to me, and when I saw it, I felt that jolt. You know, the jolt we all felt. It was just like that day. I bought it and I have it here at home. What do I do? It has to mean something. Mrs. Olsen's desk key, maybe? Please advise.

Joan read it back to herself and then read it again. Too stiff. She deleted the last sentence, changing it to *Please help.* She chewed on the tip of her thumb and held her breath.

She hit Post.

The air whooshed out of her lungs, and she slumped in her chair. Her phone made the *PING* of a text coming through.

Joan sat up and looked. Brandon. That was fast, but she shouldn't be surprised. Brandon was one of the most intense about the curse and one of her closest friends — sometimes boyfriend, sometimes just friend, and sometimes friends with benefits. You'd think that would be complicated, but it wasn't; Brandon was just Brandon.

She clicked on the message. *I'm coming over.*

She swiftly typed out a response, blowing another errant hair away from her face as she did so. *Meet me in the lab.*

Joan stood, relieved to have gotten that over with and gotten such quick results. She stretched and strode back into the kitchen with the rum, taking another long belt and then screwing the lid back on the swishing bottle as she walked. She tucked it under her arm, grabbed the blender and a carton of daiquiri mix, and headed out to her lab.

Joan made her living as a meteorologist, but she had a degree in physics — prompted, she knew, by her need to understand how a curse could fit into the Universe — and she'd built herself a lab for her experiments out in the old barn on her three-acre property just outside of town. It wasn't fancy; just some basic measuring equipment, a microscope, and plenty of dry erase boards. She was a hobby physicist, focused solely on her goal of lifting the curse.

As she approached the rustic, red-painted building, she heard a car pull up the gravel driveway and turned to see Brandon's beat-up green Honda. She tried to wave, but with her hands full, she ended up just sort of bobbing the blender up and down slightly. Then she tried to shrug ruefully and almost dropped everything. Joan hurried into the lab, nudging the door open with her foot and setting her supplies down on the rickety card table she kept next to the door.

She plugged in the blender and opened the tiny freezer at the top of her brown mini-fridge. She pulled out an ice cube tray and twisted it, plopping the frigid cubes into the blender. Joan poured in a little bit of daiquiri mix and a whole lot of rum. Then she remembered they were there to do serious work and added more of the mix, careful to put the lid on properly this time — it was one thing to make a mess in her kitchen, but the lab needed to be clean. As she hit the blend button and the lab filled with the cacophony of grinding ice, the door opened, and Brandon Barber walked in.

Brandon was Oregon-pale and dark-haired, handsome in a nerdy kind of way, with his black-rimmed glasses and his slender-but-strong physique. Joan was prone to breaking out into fantasies at the sight of his well-muscled, heavily tattooed forearms on any given day. Fortunately, he was wearing long sleeves today, in deference to the September weather.

Joan quickly moved to cover the key with a notebook. She had been giving some thought to how she could experiment on the key to uncover its secrets, and it had just occurred to her that measuring Brandon's initial reaction to it might be helpful. She hit the Stop button on the blender, and the air rang with sudden quiet.

"Can I do experiments on you?" she asked Brandon, pouring crimson cocktails into two glasses and handing him one.

"I feel like we've done this experiment before," he said, accepting the drink. "If memory serves correctly, and I'm sure it doesn't, it takes about three to get me into bed."

Joan raised a blonde eyebrow. "Since when do I have to get you liquored up for that?"

"Touchè." He leered at her. "So, what kind of experiments, then?"

"I want to measure what happens when you see the key. I felt a jolt, and I'm wondering about the energy that caused it." Joan squatted beside a cupboard and pulled out a convoluted contraption, a mass of wires connected to a clunky black helmet. She fumbled a little, her fingers tangling in the cables. "I can use this to measure your electrical pulse levels and then do the same with anyone else who comes around, and we can see how they compare."

Brandon nodded, his face sobering. "That sounds like a good start." He hesitated, biting his lower lip. "You didn't have any... symptoms, did you?"

"No. I didn't lose my voice or get blurry vision or anything. Just the jolt and then it was gone. And I haven't felt anything else looking at it or touching it."

"Okay, then! Let's do this thing. What do you need from me?"

"I just need to put this on your head and then attach some sensors to your throat and chest."

Brandon shrugged out of his jacket, baring those magnificent forearms. Joan focused on setting up her laptop, opening the program that would show the results picked up by the sensors.

"Do I need to take my shirt off or just pull it down a little?"

"Off is best," she told him. "Just the shirt, though, Barber. Keep your pants on this time."

"Fine. But under protest. Pants are the worst."

Joan looked up and grinned, taking in the view as he removed his plain black t-shirt. She used to tease him about his smooth chest, but she had to admit that the hairless expanse was ideal for displaying the intricate red and black dragon drawn across it, flying above the pine forest landscape encircling his abdomen.

She grabbed two metal-and-cork stools and positioned them near the wall in order to plug in her apparatus and then moved her computer to the side of her lab table, so she could sit directly in front of him and observe. She took a sip of her drink, shivering as the sweet iciness spread across her tongue. She set it down beside the computer.

Brandon took a seat, and Joan plunked the helmet onto his head, buckling the smooth plastic strap under his chin and pulling it snug. Next, she began positioning sticky white sensors across his throat and chest, where they would pick up his heart pulse. Her hand brushed his chest and she noticed some tension in the muscles. She rested her palm over his heart. "Are you okay? Does this hurt? Is it uncomfortable?"

"No, no. It's just — Fuck, Joan. This is so surreal. We've been working so hard for so long, and it felt like we would never find any kind of solution. And now, it's like there's this chance, out of the blue, and I'm trying so hard not to get my hopes up. Because we've *never* had any hope about this."

"I always had hope." Joan's voice was quiet as she continued her task.

Brandon laid a hand against Joan's cheek. She glanced up into his dark eyes and found herself caught in his gaze, her face on fire, in sharp contrast to his hand, chilled from his frozen drink. "But we never had any control over anything. No matter how much we learned, the ball was always in her court."

Joan reluctantly pulled away from his caress. There had been too many sessions like this in the past, where they'd been doing research or experiments and then ended up naked and distracted.

And he was right — this time they had a clue, a lead, a concrete item that they might be able to manipulate, instead of just theories. They couldn't afford any diversions.

"Okay, I think I've got you all hooked up." She stood, moving brusquely to sit down on her own stool. She turned slightly so that she was facing the computer screen, avoiding any more eye contact. "And it looks like it's picking up your electrical signals and your heartbeat." She paused for a moment to observe, watching the graph as it tracked Brandon's vital signs. "Everything looks normal for a human male of your age."

"Well, that's probably what I am, so that's good."

She glanced at Brandon, whose furrowed brow and tightly drawn shoulders belied the flippancy behind the words. She gave him what she hoped was a reassuring smile.

His charcoal eyes widened in alarm. "What? What's wrong?"

So much for reassuring. "Nothing. Just trying a new facial expression. I guess it needs some work."

Brandon laughed, some of his tension easing. "Okay, so what's next?"

Joan took a deep breath. "Now I show you the key, and we see if you feel what I felt, and how it translates into energy. You ready?"

He hesitated, pursing his lips, then nodded. He closed his eyes.

Joan reached over and grasped the spiral spine of the notebook covering the key. She pulled the notebook closer, and it dragged the key along with it. Joan scooped up the notebook, baring the key on the table.

"Open your eyes."

Chapter 3

The white line of the graph in front of her spiked wildly against its black background, and Joan jumped to her feet in triumph. It worked! She realized now that she had been subconsciously terrified that she had just imagined that jolt, but she hadn't — the key was really connected to the curse!

She spun around in place, losing her balance and plopping down right in Brandon's lap. She threw her arms around his shoulders and kissed him with wild abandon, savoring the intoxicating flavor of strawberries and rum. Everything tasted better through Brandon's lips.

She felt his arms slide around her waist as he enthusiastically returned the kiss.

After a moment, she came up for air, pulling her head back and grinning at him, and his daiquiri-stained lips twitched in response.

"It worked!" she told him.

"Yeah, I definitely felt a jolt. I mean, I was expecting it, but it still caught me off guard. Luckily, I was distracted from the traumatic memories of being cursed when you flung yourself into my lap and started making out with me."

Blushing, Joan stood up, brushing herself off. "Right. Sorry. Got a little carried away."

"No need to be sorry. Did you get the data you needed?"

"Crap!" Joan bent and looked at her laptop. "I got the data from the moment you saw it, but I would have liked to have been able to monitor the after-effects."

"Why can't you?"

"Because now what we've got is data on the effects of a woman landing in your lap and kissing you."

"Damn. Well, since the good stuff is already ruined, maybe we should get more of that kind of data? Just in case."

Joan picked up a dull yellow pencil and threw it in his general direction, missing by a mile. He ducked anyway, pulling off some of the sensors in the process. She sighed. "Let's just get that machine off of you. I hope we can get enough volunteers for further tests to make up for this one."

She knelt beside him and began carefully peeling the remaining sensors off his chest.

He laughed. "And I hope you can resist those volunteers."

Joan glared at him, deliberately pinching as she removed the next one. "I think I'll manage."

"Ow!"

She felt immediate remorse at her vindictive behavior. "Sorry."

Joan took more care with the rest of the sensors and then gently unbuckled the helmet and removed it from his head, running a quick hand through his soft hair to smooth it down.

Nope. That way madness lies. She hurriedly stood up, swaying at the sudden change in elevation, but somehow managing not to fall on her face, and stashed the helmet back in its cupboard. She returned to her stool to look at the data collected.

"Okay, so it's really clear right here, that this is the moment you saw the key." Joan pointed to the first spike in the graph.

Brandon leaned over her shoulder as he put his shirt back on, and smacked her in the back of the head with his arm. "Oh, shit! Sorry!"

She didn't turn around. "I'm sure I deserved it. Now we're even." She indicated the next section of the line. "Then it looks like your levels remained heightened, just briefly, after the initial jolt. See, they don't level off right away, not until two seconds later, which argues for lingering energetic transference."

He pointed to another area, his finger brushing the screen. "Okay, but then it goes back up right here."

"Yes. Well. Apparently, our kiss was also quite electrical."

His chest was against her back, and she could feel his laugh before she heard it, that deep, rich chuckle that was Brandon's alone. His chuckle had a way of wrapping itself around her like a warm, soft blanket. Then his arms wrapped around her too, and she looked down at his forearms, nestled against her belly. The chuckle and the forearms – a dangerous combination for her libido.

She swiveled to face him, gazing upward into his laughing brown eyes. He looked into her blue eyes and lowered his face. His lips grazed hers for just a moment.

Then he stepped back, grinning. "There. *Now* we're even."

Her heart racing, it took a moment for Joan to get his meaning. Wait, he'd kissed her as a joke? Well, fine, she didn't need him anyway.

She turned back to her computer, busying herself with saving their work, closing the laptop with a snap and standing to stow it in its storage spot atop a cabinet near the outlet. "Huh. You call that even? A teeny little peck like that, for my full-on make-out? Get outta here, Barber."

"Okay, okay. I'm going. Listen, babe, come by the bar tomorrow after work, once we've both had a chance to think about everything, and we'll swap notes on this key business."

She turned around again, watching him pull on his deep red leather jacket. "Sounds good."

Brandon sauntered out, and Joan flung herself back onto her stool, folding down over the table, resting her forehead on the hard stainless steel. This was ridiculous. They had five months left to break this curse, and she couldn't seem to keep it in her pants.

She sat up and picked up the key, holding it tightly, memorizing its jags with her fingers, hardening her resolve to concentrate solely on it until the solution was found. Yes, Brandon would be helpful with the work, but others could help too. A buffer — that's what she needed. In fact, the others were probably clamoring to get in on it. She grabbed her phone out of her back pocket.

Yep, there they were: texts from Veronica, Derek, and Ed.

Joan looked at Veronica Grinner's first. *Sweetie, why didn't you message me directly? I'm coming up there. I'll need to stay in your spare room, okay? I'll drive up tomorrow.*

Ugh. Who took the time to type in "sweetie" in a text message? To say nothing of all the times Joan had asked her not to call her that. It was starting to feel vindictive.

She messaged back. *I have limited space. Can't you stay with your mom?*

She checked the next message, which was from Derek Pandora, aka The Most Pompous Ass Who Ever Lived. *I've booked an immediate flight and will be arriving in Portland tomorrow. I will require the use of your lab and your home.*

Joan emitted a small groan. Another one who wanted to stay with her. Before responding, she clicked over to Ed Lockhart's message, praying he and his incessant pot smoking had somewhere else to stay. *Yo, I can drive down tomorrow if u want some help with this key. I can crash on my dad's couch for as long as I need. Lmk if u need me.*

Joan felt a pang of remorse for her unkind thoughts. Ed might be a stoner, but he was nothing if not considerate. She typed out a quick, grateful affirmative to him and then clicked back to respond to Derek.

Before she had a chance, the phone chirped and a new text from Veronica popped up. *My mother moved to Portland a couple of years ago. I'll need to stay with you, sweetie. I'll be there tomorrow afternoon.*

And that was that. Knowing Veronica, any protests would be gently but firmly deflected.

Joan shrugged and texted Derek. There would be no budging him either. *Veronica has already claimed the guest room, but you can have the couch in the living room. And yes, you can use my lab too.* She hit Send, and then typed out a brief description of the experiment she had run on Brandon as well, omitting everything after the initial spike of energy, and making a mental note to erase that data from her computer. Derek was a renowned neuropsychologist; hopefully he would be able to expand on the experiment and provide more nuanced equipment.

Yawning, Joan stood, stretched, and switched off the lights. She wandered back into the house to feed her cat, Friday, and rummage in the fridge for her own dinner. She settled on a slice of only-two-day-old sausage and mushroom pizza and the rest of her daiquiri and then ambled off to bed.

Chapter 4

Joan had an uncharacteristically restless night, forever fidgeting and flipping over as sleep eluded her. After an hour and a half, she drifted off, only to flounder awake as Friday walked across her face. She groaned and spent another two hours staring at the wall and occasionally scratching Friday's ears, as demanded.

Finally, around 3am, Joan sank into anxiety dreams, chased through Alexandria Elementary School by a Mrs.-Olsen-shaped pillar of flame, forced to leap over Brandon-shaped hurdles along the way. She was pulled out only by the blaring of her alarm at 7:00. Her left arm was tucked under the pillow and remained asleep.

She lurched out of bed, slapping feeling into her arm with her right hand, wincing at the spreading prickles as it slowly regained perception. She wandered into the blue-tiled bathroom, shedding pajamas across the floor as she walked.

Joan emptied her bladder and pushed aside the stiff white shower curtain. She turned the tap and tugged on it, watching as the nozzle above sputtered and then erupted. She let it run until it steamed and then stepped under the spray.

She missed the days when her job consisted solely of analyzing the atmospheric conditions and predicting rain or shine — just science. Science was what she'd signed up for.

Then the vapid "weather girl" had run off with a rogue anchorman and her boss had decided that, since his meteorologist was also a buxom blonde, he might as well put her on camera. So now she had to actually make an effort to look nice, showering every morning, wearing professional clothing and *make-up.* It was a nightmare.

Work fared little better than sleep — she spilled coffee on her keyboard, mixed up her forecasts for this week and next and had to redo the entire teleprompter program, and then stumbled over the words again during the taping. Thankfully, the station she worked for didn't broadcast the weather report live anymore, and after twelve takes, she finally wrapped up, muttering something to her boss about a sore throat to lay the groundwork for probably calling in sick the next day.

She headed straight to the bar where Brandon worked for a much-needed drink.

As soon as she entered the dimly lit room, Brandon hailed her. "Hey, babe! I'm so glad you're here! I've got a gazillion thoughts!"

She wove her way between rickety bistro tables and sturdy pool tables to her habitual green-cushioned stool at the bar. This time of day, between happy hour and the after-dinner crowd, the place was deserted. "Don't call me that. Can it wait like eight minutes? I need a drink."

"I guess so. What're you drinking today? Red wine?"

"No. Gimme a Hendrick's and soda with a splash of lime."

"The good stuff, huh? Rough day?" Brandon leaned in over the bar, as if to kiss her. Automatically, Joan began to lean in too, but then she remembered last night's resolve and her ominous dream, and she veered downward, bending over to hang her purple crossbody purse on a hook underneath the protruding dark wood counter, fidgeting with the strap and the brass hook for a long moment to give him plenty of time to get the hint.

By the time she figured it was safe to come back up, Brandon was mixing her drink, scooping ice into a glass with a clink, then grabbing the squat black bottle of gin from among the rows of bottles behind him. He poured a stream of liquor into the glass, squeezed a fragrant half-lime over it, and topped it off with fizzy soda water from a blue nozzle.

His grey flannel button-up shirt was rolled up to the elbows. Joan averted her eyes, watching an errant drop drip down the side of the tumbler as Brandon reached to his right for a lime wedge and perched it on the rim. He tossed a cream-colored cardboard coaster in front of her, advertising a local distillery, and then set her cocktail in its center.

"This oughta help."

She sipped her drink and briefly closed her eyes in bliss at the tart combination of lime and gin, the fizzy joy of the soda water. "Yum. Thank you. Yes, it's been a rough day. I just couldn't focus, you know? And I couldn't sleep last night. Like, at all."

"Me neither. Has it been eight minutes? Can I tell you my thoughts now?"

Joan smiled. "Go ahead. What are your thoughts?"

As though a switch had been flipped, Brandon shifted instantly into what she had long ago labeled his Intense Mode — he leaned forward again, supporting his body with folded arms braced against the end of the bar, his mind turned inward, and his whole face glowed. As he spoke, his voice emerged slightly breathless.

"I've been thinking about the data you pulled from me last night. My electrical current spiked, right? And then it went right back down again before you kissed me?"

Joan nodded, basking in his radiance. "Right. After a couple of seconds, it started to fall again."

"Yeah! So it occurred to me that that contradicts the documented phenomena from experiments with witchcraft.

Typically, in those cases, the subject's vitals are altered for a much longer time, and the electrical energy dissipates really gradually."

Joan put her elbow on the bar, resting her chin on the back of her hand. "So you're saying that the effects of the key aren't spell-related? Does that mean the key isn't connected to the curse after all?"

"Well. You know how I've always felt like our picture of witchcraft is incomplete."

"Oh, Brandon, not this again."

He scowled. "Look, there are hints in all of the older texts on witchcraft that there are multiple sources of energy and different types of magic that can be used! And all of the studies done on witchcraft have used the same garden-variety Wiccan style of spells. Maybe there's something else out there and that's what Mrs. Olsen used on us."

"Hints are not concrete evidence! It's just conspiracy theories. That's why we've focused our research on 'garden-variety Wicca' and probably why the scientific community as a whole has done the same. We can't go chasing wild hares — we're running out of time!"

Brandon turned away from her, grabbing a polishing rag and angrily attacking the water spots on a pint glass.

"But the curse didn't follow the same formula as a Wiccan spell either!"

"So she improvised! There's no proof that these other branches of magic exist at all, much less any information on how to find them or use them."

Lips pursed, Brandon set down the pint glass and crossed his arms. "Fine. Yeah. You're the scientist."

Joan forced her voice into gentler tones. "Isn't Veronica a witch? Maybe she can add some insight to this."

"No, she's just New Agey. She is an energy worker, though —
Reiki, I think. So we can compare those energies." He hesitated.
"I do have a... friend who is a witch. I could see if she'd be up for
helping out."

Friend? "What was that?"

"What?" Brandon began vigorously wiping down the bar,
scrubbing away an imaginary stain. He peeked at her through his
eyelashes.

Joan frowned, eyes narrowing. "That hesitation. You dithered."

"I did not."

"You absolutely did. Why have I never heard of this friend? We
talk about witchcraft pretty often – I would think it would come
up." She grabbed his hand, stilling it. "Are you seeing someone?"

"No!" Brandon wilted under her stare. His words slipped out
quickly, like fish frantic to escape a net. "Not currently. We dated
for a few weeks, about six months ago. You and I weren't together
or anything at the time. I never mentioned her because it seemed
like borrowing trouble but now we have this key and—"

"Whatever." She pulled her hand back and waved it in the air,
dismissing his fumbling disclaimer. Who needed Brandon and his
daiquiri lips and delicious arms anyway? She eyed the pentagram
tattoo just below his left elbow. He'd gotten it recently — was it
six months ago?

Focus! Joan shoved her jealousy into a tiny box and locked
it away. "It's fine. It's none of my business. If she can help,
that's what counts. Tell me about these witchcraft studies you
mentioned. Who is running them?"

"Derek has been very involved, actually."

"Well, that's good news. Derek is flying in today. And crashing
on my couch."

Brandon grinned. "Sort of a good news/bad news situation
there. What time is he getting in?"

"Actually, I have no idea. I haven't heard from him since his initial text. Veronica has been texting all day long — constantly. Way more than she needed to be. She's apparently at my place now; I left a key out for her this morning. She claimed the guest room right away, of course. And Ed is on his way down from Seattle. Thankfully, he's staying with his dad."

"I feel like Ed is the only one out of that group who I could stand staying with me," Brandon remarked.

"Well, the others bullied their way in. I've had a few comments on my post too, from people still living nearby and willing to help out. I figure I'll get them all to sign up for time slots to come in and measure their jolts. You'll come by after your shift, too, right?"

"Of course." A gust of wind struck from behind her as the door was thrown open. Brandon leaned to his left to look past her at whoever was entering. "Sadie! Get your ass over here!"

Joan swiveled on her stool to face her oldest friend, who bounced onto the seat next to her. No sooner had she sat down than Sadie was on her feet again, standing on the brass rail, leaning over the bar to plant a kiss on Brandon's proffered cheek while somehow simultaneously managing to shed her forest green coat and matching hat, depositing them onto the stool on her other side. Then she plunked back down, spun in a full circle, and stopped herself by grabbing Joan's blue-clad shoulder.

"What a beautiful day, you guys! Have you been outside? The fall is my absolute favorite!"

Joan laughed. "You said that about summer just a few months ago."

"Oh, but fall is here now, and it's the best, at least until it starts raining nonstop! Joanie, my love, you look positively exhausted." Sadie accepted a glass of white wine from Brandon with a wink and then turned her full, formidable attention back to Joan.

Used to such scrutiny, Joan merely sipped her cocktail. Sadie was the only one who was allowed to call her *Joanie*, and she was even willing to overlook *my love,* based on the force of their friendship. At least it wasn't *sweetie.* "I'm not exhausted yet. You must be looking into the future."

"Oooooh, what's happening in the future?" Sadie absently tugged at a lock of her chestnut hair with her ring-laden right hand and drummed the long blue-painted fingernails of her left on the base of her wine glass.

Joan often wondered what would happen if Sadie ever tried to sit absolutely still. Maybe she could convince Veronica to give her a yoga lesson — she was probably no crazier than the celebrities Veronica usually taught. "Absolute chaos."

"That sounds amazing!"

Brandon intervened. "Didn't you see Joan's post? About the key?"

"No, I haven't been online today. I have a life. What key? Oh! Are the two of you back together? Moving in? What key?" Sadie's head oscillated as she tried to look at both of them at the same time.

Joan rolled her eyes. "Sadie, aren't you at all concerned about the doom that is potentially descending upon us in five months?"

Sadie deflated. "Oh. This is about the curse. I should have known. Don't you guys think about anything else? You are young and vibrant and sometimes in love. You *should* move in together! I mean, look, who knows if ol' what's-her-name really meant the whole 'you'll see me again' thing, or if she even has the power to bring it around a second time. Or she could be dead. Or—"

Brandon rapped his knuckles on the bar. "Wake up, Sadie! This is important!"

Joan shook her head at him. That was no way to get through to her. She laid a gentle hand on Sadie's arm. "We have to try. Not just for our own sakes. For our families."

Sadie sobered immediately. She jumped to her feet and began to pace. "I do know that. I'm not completely in denial. I made my mom promise to take the kids if anything happens to me. I just don't see why we shouldn't have fun in the meantime! Especially if our fun-time is limited. I mean, look at you guys." She gestured widely, nearly smacking Joan in the face. "You've put your whole damn lives on hold, and you're no closer to finding a solution than when we were seven!"

Joan and Brandon exchanged glances. "Actually—" Joan began.

"We have a lead!" Brandon burst in. "Joan found an old key that gave her the same jolt as the curse did, and we're going to study it, and all the others are coming into town, and we're totally going to figure it out!"

Sadie stopped pacing and twirled around on the balls of her feet, arms lifted in triumph. "Holy fuck, you guys! That's amazing!"

Joan grinned at her. "So you'll help? I need a buffer between me and Veronica, to say nothing of Derek."

"Ugh, Deadly Dull Derek is coming?" Sadie rolled her eyes. "You're on your own there. I like Veronica, though. She's got spunk."

The door opened again and a couple walked in, hand in hand, choosing an out-of-the-way table on the other side of the room. Brandon hurried over to take their orders.

Sadie plopped herself back onto her stool, windmilling her arms as she almost overshot the seat. She leaned close to Joan and spoke in a conspiratory tone. "Don't think you're fooling me for a moment. You are perfectly capable of handling Veronica and Derek. You want a buffer betwixt you and hunkalicious over there."

"We kissed last night." Joan took a sip of her drink. "Twice."

Sadie squealed. "I knew it! I could feel the sexual tension the moment I waltzed into this place! You two are totally getting back together and you're gonna get married and have babies and—"

"Shhh! Keep your voice down!"

"Oops!" Sadie giggled and lowered her voice again. "Well? Are you back together?"

"No! We have to focus on this key! We're working on a serious deadline now. It's not like when we were twenty-four and just making out over our research, confident that we'd be finding a cure soon, but not too concerned, because it felt like we had a million years." Joan paused. "Also, some witchy ex of his is going to come help us out."

"Why, Joanie, I didn't know you had a catty side to you!"

"What's catty? Oh, no, I mean, she's an actual witch. Wiccan. She's going to help us with our experiments."

"Oh. Well, anyone with or without eyes can see Brandon is insane about you. I'm sure she was just a blip."

Brandon returned to his station, and Sadie turned to him, a mischievous smile blossoming. "So, Brandon, Joan tells me—"

"I'm sure she did," he interrupted, grabbing two pint glasses from beneath the bar. The tap hissed as he filled them with amber beer. "But she's right. We need to focus right now." He bustled back to his other customers with their drinks.

Sadie shrugged, finished off her wine, and fished some money out of her pocket. She tossed it onto the bar and reached for her coat. "Well, I gotta go pick up the twins from play practice. Should I come by this evening and help out?"

"Please." Joan's phone chirped and she grabbed it, absentmindedly leaning her cheek toward Sadie for the inevitable goodbye peck.

As Sadie bounded toward the exit, Joan read the message from Derek. "That presumptuous little fuck!"

Brandon rounded the corner of the bar, setting down his now-empty tray. "What's up?"

"He wants me to pick him up at the airport. As soon as possible. Apparently, he was expecting me to already be there. Even though it's two hours away and he never told me when his flight was getting in. And I'm not his lackey."

She angrily punched in a response. *Not gonna happen, dickface.*

Joan's finger floated above Send. Then she sighed and deleted it. She was going to have to put up with him in her house for who-knows-how-long. Might as well start out on a diplomatic foot.

Her thumbs moved furiously across the screen as she typed a new message. *I don't have time to drive up there. Take the damn bus.*

She pursed her lips and deleted the *damn*. That was as diplomatic as she could be. She sent the text.

The reply came in immediately. *I'll look into it. See you later this evening.*

Huh. No argument? Maybe Derek wasn't as stuffy as she'd always thought.

"That was unexpectedly easy. He's taking the bus."

"Who is? Derek? Doubt it."

"No, he said—" She was interrupted by the sound of another text. It was Beth Fiorelli, the notorious screamer, who had surprisingly not contacted her before now. *I'm driving up to Portland to pick up Derek. What's your address again?*

Of course — he knew he could count on other lackeys. She texted back her address and set her phone on the bar again. She knocked back the rest of her drink. She'd put it off long enough; it was time to go home and get Veronica settled in before she had to deal with even more of them.

CHAPTER 5

Joan drove slowly up her long driveway, gravel crunching under the tires, a few early red and orange leaves drifting down onto her windshield, and braced herself for Veronica's presence. They had done a lot of texting, emailing, and even video-chatting about the curse through the years, but she hadn't actually seen her since high school. Veronica had moved to Los Angeles immediately after graduation, studying yoga and other such hippy-dippy subjects and eventually gaining status as a guru to the stars.

It's so much harder to avoid someone in person — you can't just tell them you have to go and then log off or hang up. To say nothing of the added potential for punching them in the face if they call you *sweetie* one more time.

"New Agey," she muttered. "I don't deal well with New Agey."

Joan parked her red Kia behind a blue SUV and turned off the engine. A dreamcatcher hung from the rearview mirror, and a bumper sticker read *Meditation is for Lovers*. A luggage rack on the roof held six yoga mats, arranged in a pyramid.

As she gathered her belongings and her patience, she gazed forlornly at the house, usually a bastion of peace and solitude. It still looked so tranquil from the outside. She'd take a moment to enjoy it.

She savored the quiet as long as she could justify doing so and then exited the car and strode to her front door. She turned the key, twisted the knob, and opened the door just a crack, listening for any suspicious chanting or flute-playing or whatever other nonsense these New Agers got up to.

Instead, she heard a dog barking. She frowned and pushed the door all the way open. She stepped into her entryway and closed the door behind her, kicking off her black flats. "Hello?"

The door to the spare room opened and a giant fluffy white dog bounded through it, followed by a slim, busty woman wearing baby blue high-waisted yoga pants and a clinging bright yellow midriff-baring half shirt.

"What the hell?" Joan shoved the dog away as it rushed her legs. The animal began to run back and forth between Joan and Veronica, barking excitedly, nails clicking on the hardwood floor.

Veronica glided toward Joan, navigating dog-infested waters with ease, a broad smile spread across her perfectly symmetrical face. Her long auburn hair was pulled back in a loose ponytail and her feet were bare, her toenails painted the same sunny shade as her top. She spread her arms for a hug.

"Sweetie, it's been too long!"

"Don't call me that." Joan put up one hand to ward off her guest, keeping the other low in case the dog attempted another breach. "Sorry, I'm really not a hugger. And who is this great white beast here?"

"Oh, I'm sorry. Would a handshake be all right?"

"What? Sure, fine." She swung her arms, moving her right hand up into shaking position and thrusting the left down to push back the fluff monster. Veronica's handshake was pleasantly firm, and her fingernails matched her blue yoga pants.

"It's wonderful to be here, sweetie; you have a beautiful home. Such a welcoming environment, and the grounds are just gorgeous."

"Thanks. You know you didn't say you'd be bringing a dog."

"Didn't I? Well, I don't go anywhere without Willow." She knelt to address the dog head-on, giving her neck a vigorous scratch on either side. "Isn't that right, you big fluffy girl?"

Joan recoiled in horror as she watched Willow lick Veronica's entire face in one circular sweep of her tongue. Veronica laughed and stood back up. "I do hope it won't be too inconvenient for you?"

"Well, I don't think my cat will be very happy."

"Oh, you have a kitty? Willow adores cats. I'm sure they'll get along wonderfully."

"Yeah. I'm sure." Joan glanced around, but Friday was nowhere to be seen. "Um, anyway, I've had kind of a long day, and I'm sure you must be hungry and tired after your drive. What do you say to ordering some Chinese food?"

Veronica frowned. "I'm sorry, but that will be unacceptable. I'm very strict about what I put into my body."

"Sure. How about pizza? Or burritos?"

Veronica gently grasped Joan's arms and leaned her forehead against hers. Joan found herself looking cross-eyed at Veronica's slender nose.

"I hope I don't offend, but I'm afraid there won't be any ready-made food available in this rather provincial town that will suffice."

Joan leaned back and shook her arms free of Veronica's grip. "What do you propose?"

"I did take the liberty of stopping at the grocery store on my way in, and your kitchen is now stocked with wonderfully nutritious fare. Why don't I just whip something up for us, sweetie?"

"Don't call me that. Fine, as long as I don't have to cook, I'm not picky."

"Wonderful!" Veronica skipped off to the kitchen, Willow at her heels.

Joan stared after them. "You grew up in this 'provincial town,' same as me," she muttered. She pulled her phone out of her purse and texted Sadie. *She doesn't eat burritos, she brought a gigantic dog, and my forehead is no longer a virgin.*

Joan headed down the hall to her own bedroom, calling out softly, "Friday? Here, Friday. Where are you, Friday?"

A soft meow came from behind the ajar door of the hall linen closet. She pushed it open and the calico jumped into her arms from her nest of towels. "Oh, I know, kitty. This is the worst, huh? It's gonna be okay. Let's go in here."

She carried Friday into her bedroom and shut the door. She set the frustrated feline on the bed and opened the window just wide enough for the cat to come and go, shivering a little as a brisk breeze swept in. "See? We'll just keep this open and you won't have to go into the rest of the house at all! Isn't that nice?" Friday butted Joan with her head and she smiled and scratched her ears. "Okay, I gotta get changed, because if I have to wear this damn skirt for another second, I'm gonna kill someone."

Joan pulled her purse over her head and slipped off the offending pencil skirt and emerald green blouse, exchanging them for a comfortable pair of jeans and a vintage-soft burnt-orange tee emblazoned with a cartoon atom. She went into her bathroom to wipe off her make-up and vigorously brush out the ridiculous curls that the stylist at work always insisted on putting in her hair, cursing each time the brush tugged at her scalp.

Feeling like herself once more, Joan strode back into the bedroom and checked her phone. Good, Sadie was on her way. She looked at the time. Brandon wouldn't be here for another hour or so. She stuck the phone in her back pocket, gave Friday a few more minutes of love, straightened her shoulders, and headed to the now-fragrant kitchen, arriving to find Veronica emptying a can of lumpy coconut milk into a sauté pan full of colorful veggies. Willow rushed to greet Joan and she stuck out a foot to keep her away, hopping into the room and leaning against the doorframe, leg still extended.

Veronica looked up, setting down the can and picking up a slotted wooden spoon to stir. "Oh, you look much more comfortable now, sweetie. Do you feel better?"

"Don't call me that. Yes, I feel much better, thank you."

"Wonderful! Do you have any ground turmeric?"

"Any what?"

"Turmeric. The spice?"

"I think I have some taco seasoning."

Veronica winced. "Never mind."

Joan narrowed her eyes and hopped forward, pushing Willow before her. "Listen, you judgy little—"

Veronica interrupted. "No matter! I'll pick some up tomorrow. Tell me what you've discovered about this key!"

Attention diverted, Joan leaned her butt against the round four-person kitchen table and explained about the jolt, the experiment she ran on Brandon (again omitting the ultimate outcome), and Brandon's theories about the connection to witchcraft.

"Wow," breathed Veronica. "Is it really just like — that day?"

Joan shivered. "Exactly. It's unreal. We'll run the test on you after dinner, and everyone else as they arrive. I'm sure Derek will have some thoughts on how to improve the test and maybe the equipment to measure brain waves and other vitals too. The only equipment I have just measures electrical impulses, which is helpful but doesn't paint a complete picture."

Veronica waved a blue-tipped hand. "I don't know about all this science stuff! I'm really more of a mystic."

"That's actually fantastic because I'm clueless about that side of it. We're lucky to have such a broad range of experts. I know Brandon will want to talk to you about how the energy source you use in your healing work compares to that generated during Wiccan spellcasting. He's also going to try to get a Wiccan friend of his to come and talk to us about how spells work."

Sadie skipped into the kitchen, followed by her eleven-year-old twins, Becca and Marlon, who gasped with delight and ran straight to the dog.

"Ooh, spells? That sounds like fun!"

Joan lowered her foot as Willow turned her attention to the new, much more attentive humans.

"Mrs. Connor says witches are taking over the country, driving out God-fearing Christians," said Becca, looking up from vigorously petting Willow. "She says they dance around naked and stuff."

Marlon's eyes widened. "Really?"

"No, Marlon, they don't do that, and even if they did, they wouldn't do it in front of you." Sadie laughed, shedding her coat and hanging it on the back of a slatted chair. "Becca, I'm gonna get you a pentagram necklace to wear next time you visit Mrs. Connor; that oughta shut her up. Why don't you guys take the puppy outside and play for a bit?"

"Okay!" The children happily pushed Willow out the back door.

"Who the hell is Mrs. Connor?" Joan asked, lips twitching.

Sadie bounced over to the fridge and opened it up, grabbing a bottle of white wine. "This nosy neighbor who thinks I'm raising my kids to be heathens. I mean, she's not wrong, but I don't see why it's any of her business. Nice to see you, Veronica."

"It's wonderful to see you too, sweetie!" Veronica hesitated, arms outstretched. "Are you a hugger?"

"Bring it in!" Sadie set down the bottle on the counter and embraced Veronica, as Joan rolled her eyes and walked over to the stove to poke at the contents of the pan. It smelled divine, redolent of ginger and black pepper. There was another pan on the back burner, and she peeked in, lifting the lid an inch, to reveal brown rice. She wrinkled her nose.

Veronica approached. "Shall we dish up? It should be ready. Sadie, will your wonderful children be joining us?"

"No, we stopped for burritos on the way. I will have some, though."

Joan cleared her throat to cover a snicker, then pulled down three bowls from a cupboard. She claimed a smallish share of the suspiciously healthy food, scooping in as little of the brown rice as possible without giving offense and then heaping on the veggies.

Sadie danced around the kitchen, busily opening wine (she was one of the twelve people in the world who could use the bewingèd corkscrew properly), pouring two glasses ("None for me, sweetie," said Veronica. "It's sheer poison for body and mind."), and setting utensils and mismatched cloth napkins on the table.

Joan sat down and tentatively ate a slice of carrot, the complexity of the sauce rolling over her tongue, creamy, slightly spicy and full of flavor. She eagerly speared some sweet potato and onion on her fork. "Veronica, this is amazing!"

"Thank you — it's my own recipe." Veronica sat down across from her, Sadie plopping into the chair between them.

Joan took a third bite, braving the rice this time, which actually meshed well with the veggies, its nuttiness complimenting the spices. Then she glanced at Veronica. She wasn't eating, just fidgeting with her fork and staring into her bowl. Joan narrowed her eyes and looked from the chef to the food. "Why aren't you eating it? What's going on?"

Veronica bit her lip and dropped her fork, nervously pulling at her ponytail. "I have to tell you guys something. I should have said it before. It's been going on for a couple of weeks now."

Joan set her fork down and picked up her wine glass, sipping the bright, citrusy pinot gris. Sadie kept eating, but cocked her head to the side, her eyes fixed on Veronica's face.

Veronica took a deep breath and let it out slowly, gazing down at her bowl as though it was a crystal ball with all the answers. She picked up a piece of carrot and then dropped it again, wiping her fingers on her blue-and-green plaid napkin. Finally, she spoke, her voice low.

"I have been getting symptoms again. Curse symptoms. Here and there."

CHAPTER 6

Joan and Sadie gaped at Veronica. Joan opened her mouth to speak, couldn't think of anything to say, and snapped it shut. Then a rush of questions slammed into her mind and she opened her mouth again, but there were too many and none emerged as a front-runner. She whimpered.

Veronica lifted her head, eyes darting from Joan to Sadie and back again. "I know I should have said before or posted it online. But I wasn't sure. It started a couple weeks ago. I was waiting to see if a pattern formed before I told anyone about it, so I could be sure I wasn't just inciting panic for no reason." Her voice was pleading, her face begging them not to be angry. She picked up her fork and took a bite of her meal, chewing slowly. She swallowed and continued.

"And then you posted about the key, and I figured it would be best to tell the group in person." Veronica paused for another bite. "And it was so scary, you guys. I just— I didn't know how to talk about it." She put her fork back down and stared at the table, braced for reactions.

Sadie put a hand on Veronica's arm. "It's okay. Tell us exactly what's been happening."

"Well, you know the curse hit me worse than a lot of people. I fainted and then went totally blind and mute for almost four days, no breaks, no whispering, nothing."

"You, Beth, and Ed were hit the hardest," Joan nodded. "But you're not blind or mute right now, are you?"

"No. It comes and goes this time. And it's preceded by a headache. A migraine."

Sadie snorted. "Just like Mrs. Olsen had."

"How long does it last?" Joan began to eat again, automatically, her eyes remaining fixed on Veronica, who also took sporadic bites as her tale unfolded.

"The migraine starts about an hour before the . . . other stuff, so I have time to get to a safe place. The first time it happened was September eighth. The migraine hit fast. I was just wrapping up a private yoga class. I managed to get through the cool-down and see my client off, and then I went upstairs to my apartment. I lay down to meditate. My eyes were closed. And then suddenly, it got... darker." Her voice faltered, and she took another deep breath and shoveled food into her mouth. She swallowed, barely taking the time to chew, and soldiered on. "You know when your eyes are closed, but you can still tell that there are lights on? It was like the lights got turned off. I opened my eyes, but the lights were still off. I tried to call out for help, and I couldn't hear myself. It was just like being cursed all over again."

Veronica stabbed her fork into her bowl again, but it was empty, the metal clinking on the ceramic vessel. She set the utensil down and pushed the bowl back, resting her hands on the table and twisting them together. She sat silent, just contorting her fingers, watching the shapes form and reform, until finally Joan repeated, as gently as she could, "How long does it last?"

"About an hour. At least that's how long the others have lasted — that first one felt like forever, and I didn't know it was coming, so I didn't note when it started. I've kept notes since then."

"Did you bring the notes with you?"

Veronica nodded. "It's been happening every few days. No particular time of day, but, like I said, I have an hour's warning. And then I text my partner to let them know it's happening, and they note down the exact time when it hits. Then I write down when it's gone." She stood up. "I'll go grab my notebook."

Just then, the doorbell chimed its two-note tune, and Joan jumped, startled. She rose to her feet as well. "I'll get that."

"I'm just gonna check on the kids." Sadie opened the back door as Veronica headed toward the guest room.

Joan hurried through her living room, her mind spinning. She opened the door to find Beth and Derek both glaring at the door as though they'd been waiting thirty minutes instead of thirty seconds.

They made a striking pair, with her pale skin and long platinum hair beside Derek's deep mahogany skin. Beth's wide blue eyes were always brimming with judgment and Derek possessed the compatible ability to look down his aquiline nose at anyone and everyone. She was dressed in a knee-length black dress and he in his trademark pristine white lab coat. They were surrounded by luggage.

"Holy crap, Derek, is all of this yours? It must have cost a fortune to check it all." Joan narrowed her eyes. "How long are you planning to stay, anyway?"

Derek pushed past her, forcing her to step aside, rolling a carry-on sized bag behind him and leaving the rest on the porch. His voice had a faint British accent. "It's mostly lab equipment. And I will stay as long as it takes. Where is your laboratory?" He glanced around, as though expecting that the door would have opened directly into the workspace.

Joan rolled her eyes. "It's out back in its own building. Your couch is right here, so why don't you set down your personal stuff, and then we'll get the equipment out to the lab." She turned back to Beth, who hadn't moved. "Beth? Are you planning to come in? Or are you a vampire and need an invitation?"

Beth pursed her lips, touching her fingertips to the silver crucifix pendant hanging below the high neckline of her dress. "No, I'm not a vampire." She entered the room, picking up her feet as though stepping over large piles of garbage, and eyed Joan's furnishings with the air of a queen surveying a peasant's cottage.

Joan glanced at the cozy room, wondering what was wrong. The wooden floor was swept and clean. The brown fabric couch and cushy armchairs were free of debris and the large antique coffee table displayed an assortment of well-kempt houseplants in its center. An eclectic collection of bookcases lined the walls, filled with tomes of every size and color. Maybe Beth disapproved of literacy.

She shrugged. Everyone knew that Beth was judgy. No point in dwelling.

"Well, come on in, then! Veronica is just grabbing some notes, and Sadie is here too for the evening. Ed Lockhart should be arriving at some point, and Brandon Barber will be coming by in about half an hour. Have you guys eaten? Veronica made dinner."

Derek fixed her in a stern look. "And are you and Brandon currently sleeping together?"

Joan's smile froze. "What?"

"I only ask because I need to know if you will be distracted."

"No, no. We'll be plenty focused on the key." She scowled into his face, parrying his piercing eyes with her own set of matching none-of-your-business daggers.

Derek raised an eyebrow, clearly unconvinced. "See that you are. This is important."

"I'm not seeing anyone," Beth put in. "I am fully dedicated to breaking this curse."

"I wasn't worried about you." Derek returned to the door and gestured toward the remaining luggage. "The rest can go to the laboratory."

"All of it? Okay." Joan squatted to lift a hard-cased box. It felt like it was full of unabridged dictionaries. She set it back down with a thump. "Maybe I'll just grab a dolly from the garage." Grateful to flee the scene, she jogged across the driveway and rummaged around in the dusty garage for her folding hand truck among landscaping equipment and boxes of Christmas decor.

She quickly found it leaning against the concrete wall, next to an enormous inflatable Santa Claus that she always meant to put on the roof each December, but somehow never made it up there.

As she carried the dolly back toward the front door, she heard shouting from inside the house. She paused, unsure whether it would be best to dawdle in the hopes of missing the argument or hurry to intervene.

CHAPTER 7

As Joan waffled, the sound of a car coming up the drive diverted her attention. Delighted for an excuse, she turned to wait for the newcomer to arrive. She squinted into the bright headlights, trying to see if it was Brandon or Ed. She couldn't see the shape or color of the car, but she noticed a column of smoke wafting from the driver's side window. So that would be Ed.

She waved and a hand emerged from amid the haze and gave a jaunty greeting in return. He pulled in behind Beth's sedan and opened up his door. Fast food wrappers cascaded out and Joan heard a mild curse in a familiar tenor voice. She strode forward to help him clean up and began shoveling the foil and cardboard containers back onto the floor of the car, covering the cartoonish five-pointed leaves adorning the black rubber floor mats.

"Doesn't all this junk tend to get under the pedals? Maybe we should put them on the passenger side. Or in a trash bag," she suggested.

"Naw, it just makes life more interesting."

"Right, but you might hit someone."

"Naw." Ed took a drag on his joint and offered it to Joan. About to decline, she glanced in the direction of the house, where she could now hear three distinct voices rising in anger, although not quite loud enough to make out the words.

"Yeah, okay." She brought it to her lips and inhaled deeply, pulling sweet-tasting smoke through her mouth and into her lungs. She didn't smoke often and it had been a few months since she last had, but she managed to hold it in for a couple of seconds and release it without breaking into a coughing fit. She felt herself relax slightly, her mood elevating just a bit, and she offered Ed the joint again.

"Naw, you finish it off. I'm good." Joan hesitated and then took another hit. She looked around for somewhere to put it out and settled for rubbing the ember on the red hat of a creepy garden gnome that her father had insisted on placing next to the driveway. She handed the remainder back to Ed, who put it in the pocket of his short-sleeved blue shirt.

He showed no signs of noticing the cold, despite lacking a jacket and any extraneous body fat.

Joan couldn't help but compare Ed's skinny arms to Brandon's. Ed had a single tattoo on his left wrist — the logo from the *Ghostbusters* movies.

"Sounds like a bit of a fracas in there. Shall we join in the fun?" Ed headed toward the door, stumbling a little as he journeyed up the four steps to the wide porch. Joan grabbed his arm to steady him, and they nearly tumbled over. They looked at each other and burst out laughing.

The front door flew open. Beth stood silhouetted in the bright doorway, arms crossed, a scowl dominating her face. "Do I smell marijuana?" she demanded.

Joan forced herself to stop giggling. "He started it."

Beth glowered. "Do you at least have the dolly? Let's get this stuff into your lab and get started."

Ed pushed past her into the house, ducking his head to clear the doorway. "Hey, take a chill pill, Beth. I haven't seen you all in ages. Can't we just have a little meet-and-greet first?"

Joan followed him inside, stopping short as she noticed Veronica and Derek standing six feet apart, staring each other down like cowboys about to draw. "Okay, what's this all about? Were you guys yelling at each other?"

Derek turned toward her, accusation written across his stern face. "Veronica has been withholding information."

"I know that. She's going to share it with all of us tonight. She wanted to have all of the facts first, isn't that right, Veronica?" Joan nudged Veronica forward.

"I have my notes right here." Veronica slapped her notebook into Derek's chest. He grasped it automatically and turned to the first page. No academic could resist a notebook, particularly one that contained data.

"What's the info you're withholding?" Ed asked.

Veronica turned toward him with a smile and loaded up another hug into her outstretched arms. "Ed! So wonderful to see you. It's been too long!"

"Yeah, for sure." Ed said and hugged her back. Joan saw Veronica wrinkle her nose as she caught a whiff of the smoke cloud that seemed to consistently surround Ed, even with nothing lit up.

She stepped back hastily and said, "The info is that I have been experiencing sporadic curse symptoms again and—"

"Hey, me too!"

Everyone in the room froze and then slowly turned toward Beth. She was standing in front of the still-open door, where she had been loading cases of lab equipment onto Joan's dolly. Her bright smile faltered as she took in their stares. "What?"

Derek stepped toward her, his eyes narrowing. "You didn't think to share this with me before? Perhaps online or in the two hours we just spent in the car together?"

"Plus, weren't you guys just arguing about it a second ago?" Ed said.

Beth shrugged. "I didn't hear what Veronica said before. And when I had the... you know, symptoms or whatever, I thought I was just having an episode. I have episodes sometimes, you know. I didn't think it was curse-related until just now. But if you're having them too, that's what it must be!"

Joan shook her head. "No, I heard three voices shouting while I was outside. What were you fighting about if not that?"

Derek sneered. "I was yelling at Veronica for not telling me about this. Veronica was yelling at me for yelling at her. And Beth was yelling at Veronica for baring her midriff."

Joan wondered if she was going to need some kind of facial brace with all of the eye-rolling she was doing. It couldn't be healthy. "Beth, have you ever considered minding your own business?"

Beth stepped toward her, finger wagging. "Now, you listen here—"

Derek sharply clapped his hands twice for attention. "This bickering is just distracting us from the issue at hand! Has anyone else gotten any kind of curse-related symptoms?"

Joan and Ed shook their heads. "Just the reaction I felt when I saw the key," Joan said. "That's just the first time I saw it, and Brandon had the same. I haven't shown it to anyone else yet."

"Right. As you requested, I have some supplemental measuring devices, so we can run further tests."

"Oh, hey, I brought some stuff too," Ed chimed in. "From my ghost hunting. EMF detector. Pendulum. Stuff like that. It's not super high tech, but it's not Walmart crap either. It's out in the car."

"Mrs. Olsen wasn't a ghost," Beth pointed out. "What good is that stuff going to do?"

"You can get ghost-hunting gear at Walmart?" Joan asked.

"Not good gear." Ed shrugged.

Derek put up a hand to forestall any more questions. "It never hurts to definitively rule out any unlikely scenarios. Thank you for thinking of that, Ed."

"Well, it's all I got, you know? I'll grab it." He disappeared through the front door, brushing past Beth as she rolled the dolly into the house, staggering under its weight.

"Okay, where is all of this going?"

"Follow me. You sure you got that?" Without waiting for a response, Joan picked up one of the two remaining boxes and led the way through the living room, into the kitchen, and out the back door. She noted that someone — probably Sadie — had cleaned up the dinner dishes and put the food away.

Sadie or her kids had also turned on the many strands of fairy lights she had strung between the house and the lab, and the yard was brightly lit.

She picked her way down the rickety wooden steps carefully, the bumpy surface of the case continually trying to slide through her fingers. She heard laughter and looked to her right, where she could see Sadie's twins tossing a stick for an enthusiastic Willow. In the lab, she saw Sadie herself busy with something on the table in front of the window.

Behind her, Beth grunted with each *THUMP* as she maneuvered the hand truck down the three stairs.

Joan turned as she heard a wail. "Noooooooooooooo!"

She jumped to catch the boxes as the entire column wavered and swayed. They pitched forward. She blocked their fall with her back, knocking the breath from her lungs in one great big whoosh, frantically juggling her own case between her outstretched arms and miraculously managing to keep it from falling too.

"Better lighten that load," she advised breathlessly as she leaned back against the dolly, struggling to retain her grip. "The walkway is gravel."

Derek stood to the side, arms folded, and observed as Joan and Veronica each added another small case to their burdens, lessening the weight on the dolly for Beth to lug the rest of the way. He followed them, unladen, down the path into the small, brightly lit lab, where Sadie was setting out drinks and arranging a display of sliced meats, fruit, and cheeses on the card table.

"Oh, sweetie, this looks wonderful!" Veronica beamed and popped a grape into her mouth.

"This looks unnecessary." Derek frowned at the open wine bottle and last night's rum (the blender and daiquiri mix had gone back to the kitchen). "And drinking while working is completely inappropriate. Remove the alcohol from this laboratory at once."

Joan snorted. "If you think I'm going to work with you without drinking, you are sorely mistaken." She picked up the rum and shook it at him as Ed entered with an assortment of small instruments packed in tattered plastic gallon-size freezer bags. "My lab, my rules. The booze stays."

Sadie smirked at Derek and lifted her wine glass over her head. "Woo! Let's get this party started!"

"Don't mind if I do," said Ed, snagging the rum from Joan and unscrewing the lid. He took a large swig and Joan gave him a broad grin and a high five.

Derek crossed his arms and glared. "Where is the key?"

Joan pointed to a small silver-colored box sitting in splendid isolation in the center of the lab table. "It's in there. Listen, we have to be careful about this, though."

"That may be the first sensible thing you've said so far." He gestured at her to continue.

"We only have one chance to measure each person's reaction. I've already seen it. No one else here has. So we need to pick the first subject, get them hooked up to whatever sensors we have, and then everyone else leaves the room so they're not compromised. Then we put it away before we bring in the next person."

"An excellent plan." Derek picked up one of the lighter boxes, carrying it to the table and opening it to reveal a wired helmet with connected sensors, similar to the one Joan had. "I will go first, so that I can assist with the subsequent tests. Sadie and Veronica haven't seen it yet?"

Joan shook her head. "Just me. And Brandon." She glanced at her phone — 7:30. "He should be getting off work about now, so he'll be here to help out soon."

Derek nodded. "Okay. You and he will handle the set-up for my testing." He strode to the jumble beside the door and indicated another box. "We'll want this one as well. Beth, please put this on the table." He gestured to two more cases. "And that one and that one. Everything else can be stacked neatly out of the way." Derek returned to the table to supervise, waiting for Beth to lug over the heavy containers.

Sadie pushed a finger into his chest. "Do you maybe want to help out too?"

He waved a hand in dismissal. "Beth is a strong, independent woman. She is perfectly capable of—"

"Get off your lazy ass and pick up a box!" Sadie roared, swinging her arm around to point at the stack. "You might be a bigshot in London, but around here everyone pulls their own weight!"

"Damn straight," muttered Joan, opening up a case as Derek reluctantly joined the others in arranging the rest into tidy towers. It held a smooth, dull grey metal box, rectangular with a square hole in one end. She peeked inside and saw a sloping lens. "What does this one measure?"

Derek looked up. "It will scan for energy fields around the body, sort of like a primitive MRI. We'll set it to take continuous photos throughout the experiment, so it'll be a progression we can watch like an animated film." He indicated the machine he was working with. "This one is for measuring heart rate and brain waves, and it will also show the electrical current so we won't need to use your machine at all."

Veronica nudged Joan aside. "We use one of these at the yoga studio for aura photography. I can hook it up."

"Thank you, Veronica. Ed, would you set up your equipment as well? Beth, I'm sure they could use some assistance." Directions given, Derek opened up his laptop, perching on a stool at the table.

Brandon's voice drifted in from outside. "Hey, Marlon, aren't you a little young to be smoking?"

"What?" Sadie shrieked and raced outside, shoving past Brandon as he ambled in, a mischievous grin on his face.

Joan raised an eyebrow at him. "Marlon is smoking?"

"Of course not." Brandon slipped an arm around Joan's waist and aimed his lips at hers.

With a glance toward Derek, Joan stepped out of his embrace and evaded his kiss, busying herself at the snack table. No point in making the guy even grumpier than he already was.

"Cheese?" she offered. She looked up and found Brandon and Derek engaged in a glaring contest. She thrust a glass of wine and a slice of cheddar into Brandon's hand, widening her eyes and raising her eyebrows at him in the universal sign to *just be cool*.

Derek emitted an explosive sigh and returned his attention to his computer.

Sadie marched back in, heading directly to Brandon and smacking his arm. "You are such an asshole."

"Sorry." He sipped his wine and set the cheese back down on the platter.

Beth paused in her set-up to remove the sullied cheddar and toss it into the small garbage can next to the table, grimacing in distaste.

"You are not." Sadie grinned and bounced off to set up her own station. She worked in a hospital lab and would be drawing blood before and after each test to observe any changes within.

Derek looked up from his screen. "If you have quite gotten the shenanigans out of your system....?"

"Yeah. Hi, Derek. Nice to see you too. The shenanigans are out. What are we working on? Hi, Veronica, Ed, Beth!"

Beth glowered briefly in his direction before returning to her task, propping one of Ed's instruments onto a tripod. Veronica smiled warmly, and Ed gave a quick salute.

Joan quickly explained the plan. Brandon pitched in to get everything ready and Derek hooked up to the various sensors.

It was all very efficient and serious, and there were no shenanigans at all, except for one minor one where Sadie spilled a teensy bit of wine on something she was setting up for Ed, but it turned out okay because it was just a pendulum and not anything electronic.

Joan had a close call when she tripped over a cord and Brandon caught her before she fell, but she managed to twist at the last minute so that he only grabbed her arm and not her rear. Really just a caper and not a shenanigan at all. Barely more than an antic.

About twenty minutes later, everything was ready. Derek was plugged into more machines than Darth Vader at his charging station and there were still more instruments pointed at him.

Joan sat behind the laptop, observing the levels of everything from brain waves and heart rate (normal) to ghost activity (none).

"Okay, everyone who hasn't seen the key, go away!" Brandon opened the door and with a wave of his arms, shooed the group out into the yard. He shut the door with a *THUD* and swept the window curtains shut. He turned back to Derek. "You ready?"

Derek nodded once, curtly.

Brandon grabbed the box with the key and lifted the lid. Keeping his body hunched over the box to conceal his actions, he shook it out into his hand and turned, holding his closed fist in front of Derek. He opened his fingers, baring the brass key.

CHAPTER 8

Derek inhaled sharply, and the lines in front of Joan spiked, just like they had with Brandon, although there were more graphs to look at now. This time, Joan was ready for it and forced herself to remain seated. Immediately, however, she heard a wild, barbaric laugh and looked around the room for the source.

Derek was staring at her with wide eyes, Brandon with a wicked grin.

The sound was coming from her. She managed to cut it off, clamping her jaw shut, locking her eyes back onto the computer screen, hoping the guys would feel too awkward about it to comment.

"Have you finally turned into a mad scientist?" So much for Brandon ever succumbing to awkwardness.

She cleared her throat. "Um. Sorry. I got a little bit excited there." Okay, damage control. Talk about what's on the screen. Use a professional, sciency tone of voice.

"Derek, your results are comparable to Brandon's, at least as far as the limited data we pulled from him. The electrical current changed in a similar way, the levels rising quickly and then lowering after two seconds. They're still higher than the baselines at this time but diminishing. Other readings are comparable as expected — heart rate, brain waves, etc. Your aura size had an inverse reaction, tightening in and now gradually expanding and its color changed as well and is still changing; Veronica will be able to explain the significance of that better than I. No ghost activity detected."

Derek gestured to the key. "Let's put that away and get Sadie in here to draw more blood."

Brandon opened the door and called Sadie back. She danced through the door. "Do I get to stab you again now?"

"And steal his life force," Joan said.

Sadie cackled.

"Aha!" Joan pointed at Sadie. "See? Evil laughs are perfectly normal, and I am not a mad scientist. Just a regular scientist, with a science laugh."

Derek frowned, rubbing the bridge of his nose. "Could we focus, please? You all seem to be very cavalier about the fact that we have mere months to break this curse!"

The smile dropped off of Joan's face, and she shook her head, lowering her eyes back to the graphs and images on the laptop, watching as levels continued to fall and the aura kept expanding, slowly shifting in color. "No, we're not. If we don't joke about it, we'll panic or sink into depression. Shenanigans are our coping mechanism."

She looked back up at Derek, eyebrows raised, defying him to deny them this comfort. He studied her for a moment. She maintained even eye contact. Finally, he nodded. "Fair enough. Carry on."

Soberly, Sadie readied her needle and sample tube. She drew blood from his left arm, filling the tube with ruby liquid, and carefully sealed and labeled it, placing it in the mini-fridge beside the other specimen, a bottle of mustard, and a can of Diet Pepsi.

Joan continued to monitor the screen until everything returned to normal and remained there for a full minute. Brandon assisted Sadie in setting up a microscope and other equipment to study the blood samples. Derek gazed fixedly at an empty spot on the wall across the room, apparently lost in thought.

At last, Joan was satisfied with the data gathered. She stood and approached Derek. "Okay, let's get you unhooked and set up for whoever's next."

"Veronica will be next," said Derek as Joan and Brandon began disconnecting him. "Then she can observe the aura photos in subsequent subjects."

"I'm going to need to head out soon," Sadie interjected. "It's a school night."

"I think your children would rather have their mother safe than worry about school." Derek frowned at her.

She advanced upon him, shaking a fortunately-empty test tube in his direction. "Don't you dare tell me—"

Joan jumped in between them. "Hey! Look, it's 8:15 now. Let's just do Veronica's test and then see how we feel, okay? Derek, you're going to need rest too. Aren't you jetlagged?"

Derek, freed from the machines, stood and adjusted his already straight lab coat. "This is important. I can handle the jetlag."

Sadie raised an eyebrow. "Uppers?"

He glowered.

"No denial, huh?" Sadie shook the test tube at him again. "Guess we'll know soon enough."

Joan bit back a laugh, lowering her head over her notebook as she jotted down her observations of the test results.

Sadie danced over to the table to prepare a needle for Veronica.

Brandon opened the door, letting in a gust of cold wind, and called the rest of the crew back in. "We're gonna do Veronica's test now, guys, if you want to help us reset."

Beth and Ed were arguing heatedly as they entered, Ed's face turning bright red as he lambasted her. "Dude, I just don't see how you can actually not believe in ghosts when you know that supernatural shit is out there!"

"I will thank you to keep a civil tongue! As far as supernatural *stuff* goes, I only know that curses are real," Beth retorted. "And that's the work of the devil! Ghosts are just nonsense."

"The devil? The devil, my ass!" Fists clenched by his sides, Ed turned to Brandon. "Back me up on this, man. 'The devil' is just a scapegoat, am I right?"

"Wow," Sadie whispered, nudging Joan. "I had no idea Ed could even get angry. It's kind of working for me."

Brandon put up both hands and backed away. "I am not getting involved in this."

"Because I'm right!" Beth raised pious blue eyes to the ceiling, clasping her hands in front of her. "Jesus has sent us this key to fight the curse and expel the devil from our lives."

"No, actually, I'm not going to bother arguing with you because you're so sure you're right that there's no point." Brandon beckoned Veronica onto the stool vacated by Derek, still addressing Beth as he deftly buckled the helmet onto Veronica's head. "Honestly, I have no idea if ghosts exist; I've been focused on researching other areas of the supernatural world. Ed seems pretty sure, though, and he has put in the time. I bow to his expertise on the subject. If I need information on fundamentalist Christian viewpoints, I'll consult you."

Joan nudged Sadie back. "Now that's the kind of well-thought-out, even-keeled reasoning that does it for me."

Beth narrowed her eyes, her face squirming as she tried to work out whether she'd just been insulted, complimented, or brushed aside. She settled on a smile. "Please do. You won't be disappointed."

Joan and Brandon exchanged amused glances as Joan took Brandon's place, sticking electrodes onto Veronica's upper chest, above her ample cleavage.

Ed fiddled with one of his instruments. "Listen, guys, can this be the last of the night? I know these tests are crucial and all, but I did drive for five hours today, and I know Veronica came from even further, to say nothing of Derek—"

"I'm fine," Derek interrupted.

Ed paused, tilting his head and studying Derek. "Uppers?"

Joan, Brandon, and Sadie collapsed into laughter, Sadie grabbing the edge of the table to avoid falling. Derek sighed, his scowl darkening.

Ed waved his hand, dismissing the issue. "Well, anyway. None of my business. All I'm saying is that I need to get some shut-eye and soon."

Joan nodded to him. "And Sadie needs to get her kids home. I agree. Let's call it a night after this."

Everyone looked at Derek. His lips tightened, but he gave a reluctant nod. "Fine. We will be starting up early tomorrow morning, however. And I don't want any arguing. And minimal shenanigans."

Sadie lifted her wine glass in a toast. "To minimal shenanigans!"

The team worked more quickly this time, and the reset only took about five minutes, after which Joan waved Beth, Sadie, and Ed out the door. Derek joined Joan behind the laptop and Brandon grabbed the box with the key once more.

He shook it out into his hand and showed it to Veronica.

Veronica took one look and keeled over, hitting the floor with a dull *THUD*.

On the screen, her vital signs flatlined.

Her aura dissipated.

And the ghost-measuring instruments suddenly showed signs of spirit activity.

CHAPTER 9

For just a fraction of an instant, Joan, Brandon, and Derek froze, staring at their old classmate in shock. Then they leaped into action.

Brandon dropped the key, letting it clatter to the tile floor, and rushed to kneel beside Veronica, feeling her neck for a pulse and then stooping to listen for signs of breathing. Joan raced around the table, heading for the cabinet where she kept the portable defibrillator she had bought after her last CPR class. Derek scooped up the key from where it had fallen, moving it across the room, in case proximity was a factor.

As Joan began to ready the defibrillator for use, Brandon started performing chest compressions. Derek grabbed Joan's cell to dial 911.

No more than ten seconds after her collapse, Veronica's body convulsed and she gasped, her lungs suddenly pulling in air.

She bolted upright, eyes wide and darting around frantically, and grabbed Brandon's shirt, pulling him off-balance. He crashed onto his side beside her and she released him, swinging her arms wildly, groping blindly at her surroundings. Her lips moved, but no sound emerged.

Joan grabbed Veronica's arms and lowered them to her lap before she did any more damage to Brandon. Derek set down the phone and joined them on the floor, helping Brandon up.

"Veronica? Can you hear me?" Derek said.

She moved her hands to his face, feeling its contours, as though confirming its reality. Her mouth snapped shut, and she nodded her head. Her breathing was quick and frightened, but her face calmed somewhat, and she dropped her hands to her lap once more. Brandon took hold of one of them to lend what comfort he could.

Derek continued his questioning. "I'm going to assume you can't see or speak. Is that correct?"

She nodded again. Tears formed in her unseeing eyes, spilling down her cheeks, and she sobbed silently.

"Do you feel any other physical symptoms at all? Headache? Nausea?"

Veronica paused, checking in with her body, then shook her head.

Joan felt tears of her own gathering, part terror and part relief. After all, cursed Veronica was better than dead Veronica, right? She stood and walked to the laptop to check her vitals.

"It's now showing signals consistent with the tests run on the two of you," she remarked quietly. Derek got up and joined her, as Brandon continued to comfort Veronica, putting an arm around her shoulders as she silently cried.

They watched the graphs, no one speaking. The levels fell slowly, exactly as they had when Derek had undergone the test.

Just when the lines reached normalcy, they heard an audible sob and Veronica lifted her head, a look of intense relief crossing her face.

"I can see! Oh my God, I can talk!"

"Veronica!" Joan gasped, rushing back to her side.

Veronica struggled to stand, and Joan and Brandon helped her to her feet. "Can you get these damn sensors off of me?"

"Yes!" Brandon and Joan began to remove the machines. Joan heard the door creak open and turned to see Derek walking out into the yard. He returned a moment later with Sadie in tow.

"Holy crap, Veronica, are you okay?" Sadie's voice was strained, her face creased with worry as she hurried toward Veronica.

"Her test didn't go quite as expected," Derek said. "She's fine now, though, as you can see, so go ahead and draw her blood."

"Are you crazy?" Joan stopped with her hand an inch from the sensor she was about to unhook, her head snapping around to stare at Derek. "She fucking died."

"She died?" Sadie spun on the balls of her feet and shoved Derek backward. "You asshole! Were you even going to mention that?"

"It's not as though you were going to take a pint of blood. Just take a sample; they would do it in an ER."

"That's different. These tests aren't diagnostic and lifesaving. Her blood is staying put." Sadie stomped a foot for emphasis and then she whirled around again, heading straight for Veronica and enveloping her in a comforting embrace.

Veronica clung to her as Joan and Brandon continued to pull electrodes off of her skin and removed her helmet, working around the hugging pair.

Finally, Veronica pulled away from Sadie. "Thank you. I needed that. These guys can't hug worth a damn."

Sadie laughed, tugging Veronica by the hand and guiding her toward the door. "You're telling me! Come on, you're gonna get some rest now."

Derek opened his mouth to protest, shutting it tightly as Sadie glared at him. He pursed his lips as he watched them leave slowly, Sadie supporting Veronica step by step.

Joan leaned against her table, arms folded. "That's the end of the night. For sure."

Derek faced her, squaring his shoulders. "You can't be serious. If anything, this highlights the need to keep going!"

The door opened and Beth charged in. "Veronica died? She died? And the curse came back? Is that true?"

Ed followed closely behind. "We're not doing any more tests, are we?"

Beth whirled, nearly colliding with him. "What on earth are you talking about? We have to find out if that was a fluke or not."

Derek cleared his throat. "Beth's right. If Veronica was having curse symptoms before this, and she had a more severe reaction to the key, we need to find out if the two are related. Beth, we need to test you next."

"Well, wait just a moment—" Beth faltered.

Ed gave a sardonic huff. "Oh, so you want to risk anyone's life but yours? Typical."

"We're not risking anyone's life at all," Joan declared. "And we're not doing anything more tonight! This is insane! Most of us are exhausted. Derek's potentially on speed. It's time for us all to take a step back, get some rest, and come back to it tomorrow morning."

"*First thing* tomorrow morning," Derek insisted.

"Fine." Ed pulled the door open with a scowl. "See you guys tomorrow."

Beth narrowed her eyes at Joan. "My coat's in your living room." It sounded like an accusation, as though Joan was a notorious garment thief.

Joan nodded once, curtly and walked out the door and back to her house. Brandon followed, Beth trailing behind. Derek remained in the lab, presumably to tidy up his instruments. Joan didn't really care what he did. She could feel all of her emotions draining into a great black hole of exhaustion.

Beth's brown wool coat was laying on an armchair and Joan picked it up and tossed it to her. She caught it and shrugged it over her shoulders. "Tell Veronica I hope she feels better. I'll see you guys tomorrow. First thing."

"Sure. See you."

Beth left, and Joan made a beeline for her favorite chair and lowered herself down onto it, sinking into the cushion. She tipped her head back to look up at Brandon. He grimaced at her and sat on the edge of the coffee table, his legs stretched out beside her chair.

"Hey," she said hollowly. "You gonna be okay?"

"I don't know, babe. That was— I don't even know what that was."

She held out a hand and he squeezed it.

His voice sounded dull and tired. "I've never given CPR to an actual human, you know. Just a dummy."

"Me too. You did great though."

"Did I?"

"She's alive, right?"

A weary smile appeared on his face. "She is. She's alive."

"You saved her. Dude! You saved a fucking life tonight!"

"I am a fucking hero!"

"You're *my* fucking hero!" Joan felt herself relaxing. She gave him a teasing smile. "You know what heroes get?"

He stared into her eyes and her heart beat faster. "Ticker tape parades?"

"No." She leaned forward, her face next to his, lips almost touching.

"Heroes get kisses," she whispered. And then her lips were on his and she melted into the kiss, completely losing herself, totally forgetting that she wasn't supposed to allow herself to be distracted.

She was rudely pulled back to reality at the sound of a throat clearing. Somehow she was on his lap again, straddling his legs.

Joan jumped up, cursing. "Dammit, Sadie, don't you ever knock?"

"Knock on what?" She laughed. "There's no door to this room. And how was I supposed to know you two would be in here necking? There are children present, you know."

Joan smiled weakly at Sadie's gaping middle-schoolers. "Sorry, kids."

"That's okay," said Becca. "When Mom was dating Seth we saw—"

"Ooookay," Sadie put a hand on each kid's back and scooted them toward the door. "We are going home now!" She handed Marlon her car keys. "Get it all booted up for me; I'll be right out."

"How is she?" Joan asked.

"She's shaken, but I think she's going to be fine once she gets some rest."

"Thank goodness. Will you be able to come back tomorrow morning?"

"Yeah, I'm working afternoon shift, so I'll be here as soon as I drop the kids off at school." Sadie grabbed Joan and Brandon's hands and guided them together. "Now, go back to what you were doing." And with a knowing grin, she was gone.

Sadie was the worst buffer ever.

CHAPTER 10

T he next morning, Joan woke up slowly, opening her eyes and stretching luxuriantly. She flipped over onto her side, only to find Brandon propped up on one elbow watching her.

She bolted up into a seated position, holding the comforter over her chest. "What the hell is your problem?"

"What?"

"You're just watching me sleep? That's so creepy!"

"Is not. You're the cutest sleeper ever. Lay down. Snuggle a while." He grabbed her shoulders and eased her back down onto her pillow. She gave in and cuddled up against his bare chest.

"Okay, if you insist. What time is it, anyway?"

Brandon craned his neck to look at the clock. "Quarter to seven."

Joan sat up again. "Crap! I gotta call into work. And we have to get you out of here before anyone else sees you. Derek will never let us hear the end of it. And we have work to do. People are going to start coming in for key testing at nine, and we should do Beth's and Ed's tests first."

Brandon sighed and stretched. "Fine. But you know me; I'm no good at rushing in the morning. I need breakfast and time to adjust to being awake."

"Yeah, okay." Joan pushed the covers back and swung her legs onto the floor. Still naked, she strode to the dresser and began to rummage in the top drawer. "Here. You can't be wearing the same clothes as last night." She pulled out a pair of men's jeans and a black t-shirt and tossed them to Brandon. "I don't have any of your underwear here; you'll have to turn yesterday's inside out."

He caught the clothing and held up the shirt. "These aren't mine."

She froze halfway into her jeans. "What the hell are you talking about?"

"Just kidding." Brandon raised his eyebrows over a broad grin. "Wow, you were really concerned there for a moment. You been keeping guy's clothes around lately?"

She picked up a shoe and threw it at him. "You're the worst. Get dressed."

As Brandon pulled on the garments, Joan grabbed her phone and prepared her fake cough, pulling up her boss's number and hitting Call. "Hey, Doug," she said, weakly. "I'm not gonna — *cough, cough* — make it in today. *Cough, cough.*"

A few minutes later, Brandon was climbing down the five-foot wooden ladder she kept outside her window for Friday to sit on.

And then suddenly he was clambering back up.

"What the hell are you doing?" Joan hissed.

"Veronica is out there! She's butt-ass fucking naked, lying in the middle of your backyard!"

Joan peered out the window. Sure enough, Veronica had spread a yoga mat on a blanket and was lying on her back without a stitch of clothing, her eyes closed, arms spread wide and legs folded up so that her knees peaked toward the overcast sky. The key rested on the center of her chest, directly between her breasts.

They gaped at her for a moment in shocked silence.

"Well, that settles it," Joan said finally. "That bitch is crazy. Come on, we'll sneak you out past Derek. He's probably still asleep anyway. He had to have been super jetlagged, right?"

"Sure. Or crashed from all the speed."

"Or he could be back up and on more speed, I guess."

Brandon shrugged. "Let's go find out."

They crept to the door, peeking into the hallway and listening for any sounds of stirring from the living room. All they heard was the ticking of the big clock in the rarely-used dining room, so they slipped out and made their way down the hall. They paused again at the entrance to the living room, but Derek lay motionless on the couch, breathing evenly.

Joan grabbed Brandon's hand and pulled him toward the front door. They got about halfway there when Derek's voice came from behind them.

"Do you have any tea?"

Joan spun around. "Tea? Yes! Or coffee, if you decide to be a normal American and not pretend you're actually from England." She gestured wildly. "And look, Brandon has just arrived to join us for breakfast!"

"Uh-huh." Derek closed his eyes again. "If it will make you feel more comfortable, I'll pretend to believe that. Just don't allow yourselves to be distracted today. And I want tea."

"Telling us you're going to pretend to believe something is not really consistent with actually pretending to believe it," Brandon pointed out.

"Well, I'll pretend it to everyone else. Is the tea forthcoming?"

Joan sighed. "Yes. We will make you some fucking tea."

Derek opened his eyes and lifted his head. "Not a morning person?"

"I usually am. You're just making me grumpy," she shot over her shoulder as she walked into the kitchen. Brandon followed, grabbing the kettle from the stove and taking it to the sink as Joan headed for the coffee-maker.

With the easy rhythm of two people who had breakfasted together many times, they began to assemble the meal, making the hot beverages, mixing up pancake batter, pulling pans from cupboards, pausing for little kisses here and there.

Brandon took Derek his tea. Then he brought it back to add milk and then returned once more for sugar, while Joan heated the griddle for the pancakes. She scooped batter into puddles, humming as she watched for bubbles and then flipped them over.

Another pan slid onto the burner beside hers and minutes later, the kitchen filled with the heavenly aroma of sizzling bacon and the sound of eggs cracking into a bowl.

Joan made a stack of flat cakes on a plate and poured more batter, smiling as she felt Brandon's arms slide around her waist. She turned for a kiss.

As his lips touched hers, however, he let out an abrupt yelp, lunging against Joan, who lurched back, slamming against the hot stove.

Joan looked past Brandon just in time to see Veronica's naked swinging hips leaving the kitchen.

"What the hell was that?" she asked.

"That randy little so-and-so just smacked my ass!"

"'Randy little so-and-so?' Are you eighty?"

Derek's voice drifted in from the living room. "What on earth? Put some damn clothes on!"

"Well, at least she managed to catch Derek off-guard," laughed Joan. She turned her attention back to the griddle, picking up her spatula. "As for you, those eggs need stirring. Get your head in the game, Barber."

The doorbell chimed. "Can you get that?" she called to Derek, assuming Veronica had retired to her room. She heard the door open and then a shriek.

Joan stuck her head around the doorway and saw Veronica's bare posterior and, beyond her, Beth covering her face with both arms.

Joan sighed, exasperated. "Veronica! Go get dressed! Beth, come on in. There's coffee, and breakfast is almost ready."

As Beth edge forward, eyes still covered, Ed jogged up the front steps, smoke rising from the joint in his hand as he pushed past her into the house. "Nice tits, Veronica. Did I hear coffee? And breakfast?"

Joan pounded on the doorframe for attention. Ed, Veronica, and Derek peered at her. Beth turned in her direction but didn't lower her arms. "Ed, there is no smoking in my house. Veronica, go and put some clothes on before Beth has a damn heart attack. Derek, come in here and help Brandon set the table for breakfast. Beth, Veronica just left the room — you're safe."

Beth cautiously peeked over the crook of her elbow, only uncovering her face when she was sure there was no sign of Veronica.

Ed ambled back outside and Derek reluctantly rose from his couch, dressed in his lab coat. Had he slept in it? How did the damn thing stay so immaculate — and unwrinkled?

Fifteen minutes later, they sat down for breakfast. Derek, Joan, Ed, and Brandon ate the bacon, eggs, and pancakes while Veronica and Beth nibbled on some fruit. To Joan's surprise, Veronica accepted a large mug of black coffee.

"It's my only vice, sweetie," she said when asked.

"Don't call me that," Joan replied.

Brandon interjected. "So, Veronica, what the hell were you doing outside on the lawn this morning without any clothes on?"

"I was meditating on the key. I placed it on my crown chakra, my third eye, and my heart for ten minutes each to see if I could gain any insight into the curse."

Derek sipped his tea. "Interesting concept. Was it effective?"

Veronica nodded emphatically. "It was! During the first session, my crown showed me the key's energetic fields. It was quite ugly, showing violent colors, and it felt sort of slimy. Then the ajna — that's the third eye chakra." She gestured toward her forehead. "There I picked up some actual images. Mostly of Mrs. Olsen opening her desk with the key, which explains where it picked up the curse energy. And one of another woman. A beautiful woman about our age — like seriously, stunningly beautiful. Except that she looked a little bit like Mrs. Olsen around the eyes. But I'd never seen her before."

"What was she doing?" asked Brandon.

Veronica shivered. "Staring at me. Just staring."

Something bleak in Veronica's tone brought a lump to Joan's throat and she set down her egg-laden fork. "What does that mean?"

"I don't know. I don't know who she was. She was only there for a moment. Then it was back to images of the desk and Mrs. Olsen."

"And the heart?" Brandon asked.

"Hate. Pure, unadulterated hate." Veronica took a big gulp of her coffee, then set down her mug and toyed with the handle. "It was awful. I have never felt so hated. But it also felt — unfocused, if that makes sense. Like it wasn't directed at me, but I was in its field of hatred. Just coincidentally."

"That could be a good sign," declared Derek. "Maybe we could shift the field away from us."

"What? And onto someone else?" Joan shook her head. "That's not okay."

Veronica held up a hand. "No, he has a point. We could shift it to an object. Maybe even the key itself. And then the entire curse would be focused onto something that is naturally blind and dumb, rather than us. It would essentially neutralize it."

"Is that possible?" Beth asked. "How would you do that without using witchcraft?"

"Well, we would have to use witchcraft, of course," said Brandon.

Beth folded her arms, her face stony. "I will not use the tools of the devil."

Veronica rolled her eyes. "Witchcraft isn't a tool of the devil, sweetie."

"As far as I'm concerned everything you just said was tools of the devil!" she shot back. "With your talk of chakras and violent energy! What is violent energy, if not witchcraft? You're messing with dangerous forces, and I just hope you turn back to Jesus before it's too late for your soul!"

"I wasn't messing with the violent energy, you prissy little-"

"Hey, now." Ed stood up, spreading his arms to separate the two women. "There's no point in getting our aglets in a twist."

"Aglets?" Joan frowned. "Isn't that the hole your shoelaces thread through?"

"Is it? A lady I used to know always said it. I thought it was something to do with an apron string." Ed's brow furrowed as he considered the implications.

Brandon pulled out his phone and typed furiously, as the rest watched in silence. "Nope, it's actually the plastic thingy at the end of your shoelace," he corrected.

Ed turned back to Beth and Veronica. "Look, the point is that we can't be turning against each other here. Let's just agree that this curse needs to get lifted, and we'll use whatever tools we can to lift it." He held up his hand again to forestall Beth. "But we can also agree that no one will have to do anything that they find personally offensive. Beth, you don't have to do any witchcraft, okay? There's plenty of us here who can do it instead and plenty of other stuff for you to do. And on the other hand, no telling the rest of us that we need to find Jesus or any kind of crap like that. We're all adults here, and we can decide on our own religion."

"But—"

"No!" Ed pounded his hand on the table and everyone jumped. "No trying to save us from anything but the curse! We've all heard it from you before. We don't need to hear it again now."

Tight-lipped, Beth nodded.

"Good. Now, let's enjoy our breakfast." Ed sat down and began shoveling eggs and bacon into his mouth.

CHAPTER 11

Half an hour later, back in the lab, they hooked Beth up to the machines and showed her the key. Her reaction was the same as Veronica's. They were ready for it this time, though, and she hardly died at all.

After they revived her, Veronica offered to take her back into the house to rest, but she protested that she didn't want to be alone. So Joan dug a blanket out of a cabinet and Beth wrapped herself in it, seating herself on an out-of-the-way stool.

Ed picked up the helmet, examining it. "My turn?"

"Yes, that would be best," said Derek, carefully extracting the machine from Ed's accident-prone hands.

Joan objected, addressing Derek. "Ed, Veronica, and Beth were the three worst cases in the original curse — the only three who fainted and the only three who went one hundred percent blind and dumb for the full twelve hours. We already know how this is going to go. Let's spare the poor bastard his death."

"Naw, it's okay, Joan." Ed plunked himself down on the test-subject stool. "I appreciate that, but we actually don't know how it's gonna go. Beth and Veronica have both been getting curse symptoms and I haven't. We should see if there's something different about me and my connection to it."

Derek nodded. "He's right. We need this data."

She glowered at him. "Of course you'd say that. You don't care about anything but data."

"How dare you?" Derek paused in his task of buckling the sensory helmet under Ed's chin, straightened his back, and smoothed down his white coat. "I care a great deal about everyone affected by this curse, and that is precisely why I am so focused on collecting and analyzing this data. I have dedicated my life to the removal of the curse and I will be damned—" he pounded a fist on the lab table and Joan jumped, eyes widening as she stared at him — "if I'll allow you to reduce that to an episode of 'Derek the Dull and His Dedication to Data!'"

His eyes blazed and his nostrils flared as he stared at her in challenge.

Joan lifted her hands in surrender, backing away. "You're right. I'm sorry. As long as Ed is okay with it, let's run this test. I'll get the defib ready."

Derek returned to the helmet. "Thank you."

"Poetic," muttered Brandon to Joan.

"Right? Who'd have thought?"

By this time, everyone had their routines down, and it only took a minute or two to reset all of the equipment. Joan sat on the floor beside Ed's stool, ready to catch him and begin CPR. Brandon knelt beside her, defibrillator paddles in hand. Veronica tensely watched the aura-sensing machine and Derek kept his eyes on the laptop screen. Beth positioned herself in front of Ed with the key in its box, poised to open it up.

"Ready?" Derek asked the room.

There were tight nods all around, and then Beth showed Ed the key.

Nothing happened.

There was no change to Ed's vital signs, no collapse, not even a pulse of his aura. His heart rate accelerated slightly, but that would have been normal in a tense situation.

The group collectively paused, frozen and silent.

"Um," said Ed after a moment. He tilted his head, his eyes darting around the lab. "Is that it? Wasn't I supposed to feel a jolt?"

Joan scrambled to her feet. "You didn't feel anything at all?"

He shook his head, bewilderment written across his face. "Nothing."

Beth began to wail.

"What now?" Joan asked, exasperated, turning toward her.

"I must have done it wrong!" Beth declared. "This is all my fault and we won't have another chance!"

Brandon laughed and Beth spun to glare at him.

"Oh, come on, Beth," he chided, standing up and brushing off his knees. "How could anyone possibly fuck up the act of showing someone a key? It's obviously not your fault." He turned to Derek. "Is there a possibility that the instruments malfunctioned?"

Derek shook his head. "No. It's always possible that any given machine could be faulty, but all of them at once? Not likely. Besides, Ed himself said he didn't feel a jolt at all, which isn't dependent on the instruments. This must have something to do with him."

They all turned and stared at Ed. He gave a weak smile. "So I'm defective?"

"Oh, sweetie, you're not defective," reassured Veronica. "If anything, you're more fective than the rest of us!"

"More fective?" Joan raised an eyebrow.

"I mean, he's less cursed! If the key didn't trigger him like it did us, right?"

Derek held up a mahogany hand. "I wonder if this could indicate something about the key. Perhaps it's not connected to the curse, after all."

"You can't be serious!" Brandon shouted. "That jolt felt exactly the same as the curse to me. Did it feel any different to you?"

"It felt the same as I remember. But it's been nearly thirty years. Maybe we misremembered. Or maybe it's just a coincidence that it triggered something in us, and not curse-related at all. Maybe there's something else all of us have in common, which doesn't apply to Ed."

Brandon shook his head. "No. No, this is something else. Something Ed has done to distance himself from the curse's energy. Maybe something to do with his work as a ghosthunter. He's built up an immunity to supernatural energy."

"Well, wait a moment," Veronica objected. "If anyone is immune, it's me. I'm an energy healer and a yogi! I've dedicated my life to mastering my energetic self!"

"Actually," Joan said. "That might make you more open to it. You've deliberately made yourself more energetically sensitive."

"Oh." Veronica's face fell. "And I was already extra sensitive to begin with!"

"It's cool, though," observed Ed. "We can use this to figure out what I've done different and then everyone else can do it, right? This might be our answer to breaking the curse."

Veronica perked up. "That's true!"

"Meanwhile, I'm getting out of this get-up." Ed began to unbuckle the helmet, and Derek leaped to help him with the expensive piece of equipment.

"I'll get that for you."

Ed smirked and dropped his hands. "Don't want the stoner to touch your stuff, huh?"

"I don't want anyone who isn't a scientist to touch my delicate machinery," he corrected.

Brandon nudged Joan. "That's what she said," he whispered.

Joan choked down a laugh, turning it into a cough, and Derek turned a narrow-eyed glance toward her.

"Well," she said, stepping forward hastily, "I'm a scientist. So I'll just go ahead and switch off these machines since we don't have anyone else here to test."

"When will more be joining us?" Derek inquired. "And in light of this new development, I'd like to get a few outsiders in here to be tested as well, to see if they react. If they do, we will know that the curse is not actually the source of the key's energy. If they don't, we still won't know for sure, but-"

"We do know for sure," Brandon insisted, crossing his arms and glowering.

"No!" Derek snapped. "We strongly suspect it! It hasn't been proven!"

Brandon advanced upon his old classmate, stopping an inch away from him, pushing himself into Derek's personal space. "There. Is. No. Question."

Derek remained unmoving and unfazed. He studied Brandon's face. "I understand your reluctance to accept the possibility that this isn't the answer we'd hoped for. But if we blindly follow a lead that turns out to be nothing, we might miss a true clue. It is vital that we be certain."

Joan grabbed Brandon's flannel-clad arm and hauled him backward, away from Derek. "He's right. If we focus all our efforts on this key, and it turns out that the key isn't actually the answer, we've wasted our time."

He angrily shrugged free of her grasp. "Whose side are you on? I need some fucking air." Brandon stormed out of the lab, slamming the door behind him.

Joan rolled her eyes. Great time for a tantrum.

Derek pointed to Joan and then to the door. "You. Go after him."

"Me? Why do I have to do it?"

"He's your fuck buddy. Bring him back, so we can get this sorted out."

Beth gasped, her hands flying to her face. "Language! There are ladies present."

Joan flipped her off as she sauntered after Brandon. "I don't see any ladies here; just two badass bitches and one whiney one."

Veronica looked pleased to be included in the bad-ass bitch club. She followed her out into the cool September morning, catching up and throwing a companionable arm around Joan's shoulders.

Joan stepped off the path and onto the yellowing lawn to evade the other woman, raising a blonde eyebrow at her. "Not a hugger, dude."

Veronica smirked. "Don't call me that."

Despite herself, Joan laughed. "Touchè, madam."

"Listen," Veronica lowered her voice, as though imparting a great secret. "I don't think Derek has a great understanding of human nature."

Joan stared at her. "You followed me out here to tell me the most obvious piece of news since the discovery of gravity?

Veronica nodded emphatically. "I know, right? Why did it take people so long to realize that things fall down? No, but all I meant was that you're the one Brandon's annoyed at right now. So I should probably go after him, not you."

"Fair enough." Joan started to turn toward the lab, but another logistical thought occurred to her and she turned back. "And then do you want to maybe post up on the front porch and welcome the next test subjects? They should be coming by soon, and someone needs to fill them in on what's going on and send them around to the lab. You're really more of a people person than I am."

"Sure." Veronica strode across the yard to the bench under the big autumn-tinted oak tree where Brandon sat with his back toward them. Even from this angle, you could see that he was still fuming, his shoulders tense, his arms making occasional angry gesticulations to himself.

Joan sighed and went back into the lab, where yet another argument was in full swing.

"Yeah, but each time a death occurred," Ed was saying, "whether it was you or Veronica-"

"I am not dead!" Beth retorted. She grabbed his hand and flailed it around. "Do I seem dead to you?"

"You were clinically dead for a moment," Derek pointed out from across the room where he was seated at the lab table, pencil scratching as he furiously recorded his notes.

"And when you were dead, the sensor picked up ghostly activity!" Ed pounded a hand on the card table, and it collapsed with a loud clatter. The bottle of rum rolled away under the lab table and Derek stooped to pick it up, holding it gingerly by the cap, away from his body, like one might hold a dead rat by its tail. He leaned across the table, placing it as far from his seat as he could, and then returned to his writing.

Joan glared at Ed and stooped to pick up the table, flipping it onto its side to examine the legs. Ed, Derek, and Beth watched as she unfolded them, shaking each one to ensure its stability. She turned it right-side up with a meaningful *THUMP.*

Ed shrugged with a rueful grin, which faded as he turned back to Beth. "Proof! Ghosts are real!"

A husky female voice drifted in from the doorway. "Well, of course they are."

The group turned and there, perfectly posed in the entrance, leaning against the side of the doorway as though a movie director had arranged her there, was the most gorgeous woman Joan had ever seen.

"Hi." The woman smiled, shifting into — how was it possible? — an even more entrancing pose, with one hand reaching to the top of the doorframe and the other on her hip. "I'm Wendy. The witch."

Chapter 12

Wendy was far too tall for comfort, even in her flat-soled black ankle boots. Her long, shapely legs were exquisitely displayed in a pair of burgundy leggings. A short black skirt hugged her hips as delicately-but-firmly as a geek holds a mint-condition new-in-box rare action figure. Her torso was clad in a red silk blouse, designed to showcase her impeccably proportioned hourglass figure – the kind rarely seen outside of a cartoon. Her caramel-colored skin was impossibly smooth and her long raven hair cascaded down her back in effortless waves.

No wonder Brandon had been reluctant to introduce her to Joan.

The group gaped at her for a gloriously awkward thirty seconds. She basked in their attention, switching poses occasionally.

Finally, Derek recovered his wits and stepped forward, hand extended. "Hello, Wendy. I'm Derek. Thank you for agreeing to help us with our research."

Her amber eyes held his gaze as she shook his hand. "Absolutely. It's a pleasure to meet you, Derek."

Derek shivered and pulled away. He stumbled a little as he retreated toward the table, never taking his eyes off the witch.

Wendy glanced around the lab. "I was expecting Brandon Barber to be here. Will he be joining us soon?"

Joan pulled herself together. She cleared her throat and Wendy turned toward her, one eyebrow raised. "Yeah, um, he's just outside, actually. I'll go and get him." She inched toward the door, unable to stop herself from babbling nervously. "I'm Joan, by the way; I'm Brandon's, um, girl— fuc— friend. We're friends, really, that's what we are. Very good friends. Been friends for years. This is actually my lab here. Welcome to my lab. I'm a physicist. It's my physics lab."

By now she was standing in the doorway, her own pose not saying 'movie starlet' so much as 'frightened and defensive badger.' She desperately looked toward her classmates. Ed and Derek were watching Wendy like mice transfixed by a cat that they really wanted to get to know better, but knew they probably shouldn't.

Beth was staring at Joan, making a frantic throat-cutting motion over and over again.

Right. Joan took a deep breath. "I'm going to go get Brandon."

She bolted out into the yard, sliding a little as she hit the gravel running. Rounding the corner, she saw that Brandon and Veronica were still deep in conversation beneath the oak tree. She hurried toward them, slowing as their earnest voices drifted toward her.

"Well, I think the two of you absolutely belong together," Veronica declared.

Joan paused to listen.

"I think so too! Joan's just so prickly, though; it's hard to know what *she* thinks."

Prickly? Her?

Joan took a big step backward and almost tripped over a branch, one foot remaining on the ground, arms and other leg swinging wildly as she struggled to regain her balance. She clenched her jaw, determined to remain totally silent, bending and contorting her body. Finally, she found her equilibrium, frozen in a crouch on the ground.

She whipped her head up to peer at the pair in front of her and silently exhaled in relief as she saw that they hadn't turned. Still crouched, she scrambled backward about fifty feet and then stood, taking a moment to compose herself into a carefully casual air. "Hey, Brandon," she called. "Your witch is here."

Brandon's head whirled around and then he relaxed as he saw how far off she was. "Crap, what time is it?"

"Nine, I guess. Veronica, would you mind heading for the front porch? We're expecting Susan Triple, Paul Shaw, and Lily McKay."

"Oh, yeah, sure." Veronica stood, stretched, and ambled toward the house.

Joan studied Brandon, unable to keep a small smile from her lips. He wanted to be with her. Take that, Wendy the Bewitching!

"What?"

"Nothing," she said. "You coming?"

"Yeah." He lugged himself to his feet and rubbed the back of his neck. "Look, I'm sorry I was such an ass back there."

"All good." She grabbed his hand and tugged him toward the lab. "So. Wendy is... striking."

"Uh. Is she?"

Without dropping his hand, Joan slapped his side lightly with her elbow. "Don't try to pull that shit with me, Barber! She's easy on the eyes and you know it. You just sound like more of an asshole if you try to act like you disagree."

"Fair enough. I broke up with her, though."

"Shut up! There's no way in hell you dumped that woman."

"I did!" Brandon stopped walking, pulling Joan around to face him. He lifted his unencumbered hand to her cheek, and her pulse raced. His eyes met hers. "Seriously. I hooked up with her right after you and I had that whole are-vampires-real fight. I was pissed, and I went to this magic shop in Salem to see if there were any books that would support my stance-"

"Your crazy stance," Joan murmured.

"Are we doing this again?"

She stepped closer to him, molding her body to his, tipping her head to gaze up at him. "Vampires aren't real. They don't make any sense."

"Joan! Can I just finish my story, please?" He leaned in, a wry smile playing at his lips.

"Yeah. Sorry. You went to a magic shop." She wrapped her free arm around his waist.

"Wendy was working there. I wanted to get back at you. So I asked her out and we went on a few dates. And then you called me up, and you were all, 'This is stupid, and it doesn't matter if vampires are real—'"

"No, I remember that," Joan purred. "What I said was that it didn't matter if *you thought* vampires were real."

"Uh-huh." Brandon stroked her cheek. "And then I broke up with her. We've kept in touch and she's been dropping some unsubtle hints about going out again, but as it turns out—" He lowered his head, his lips an inch from hers. "I prefer blonde scientists who curse a lot and drink too much."

"That's the sweetest thing anyone's ever said to me," Joan breathed, closing the tiny gap between their lips and throwing herself into the kiss, reveling in his soft lips moving against hers.

She pulled away reluctantly. "Come on. We have to go learn about witchy energy from your biggest fuck-up."

He chuckled, his chest reverberating against her body, and stepped back.

They strolled into the lab, where they found Derek and Ed attentively peering over Wendy's shoulder as she drew something on a notebook. Beth was keeping her distance, standing close enough to hear what they were saying, but obviously trying to avoid any contamination by this blasphemer.

As they entered, Wendy's head turned, and Joan saw her gaze dart straight to their joined hands. She smirked as she met Wendy's narrowed eyes.

The witch was quick, though. Almost immediately, her eyes cleared, her head tossed, and her lips widened into a smile as she rose from her stool, smoothed down her skirt, and sashayed toward them.

"Brandon, you are as handsome as ever! It's so good to see you again!" Wendy deftly inserted herself between Brandon and Joan, leaning in to kiss him on the cheek.

Brandon tried to drop Joan's hand, but she doggedly hung on, dragging him toward the table to see what Wendy had been drawing. Wendy was forced to decide between moving aside or being awkwardly herded by Joan's arm.

She chose to move to Brandon's left, linking his arm in hers and leading him to a stool beside her. Joan trailed along, still clutching his hand like a lifeline.

"Sit down, please. I've been showing these *charming* boys-" Wendy smiled warmly at Derek and Ed, who preened. "Just how a curse-removal ritual might work."

"Really?" Brandon pulled his arm out of Wendy's grasp, grabbing the notebook. "You never told me you knew how to do that."

Joan watched closely as the witch's smile faltered again, just for a split second. "Well, I've grown in my craft since we last spent time together."

"Your craft?" Beth spat. "You mean your devil worship?"

Wendy spun to face her accuser. She cocked her head as she studied Beth, her eyes lingering on the cross pendant. "I don't worship the devil. I tap into the natural energies all around us."

"You do spells."

"Yes." Wendy folded her arms and leaned her hip against the table. "And I suppose you spend your Sundays sanctimoniously praying to your oppressive patriarchal god and demigod."

Beth sputtered. "God is not oppressive, you harpy. And what the heck is a demigod?"

"Jesus is supposed to be half man and half god, right? Sounds like a demigod to me. Like Hercules."

Beth's eyes bugged and her voice broke as she shrieked, "HERCULES?"

"Okay, come on, enough baiting," Ed, ever the peacemaker, butted in. "You're both making some great points, but I don't think this is the right time for a theological debate."

"Great points?" Beth's hot a venomous glare in his direction before directing a laser focus on Wendy again. "Okay, so you 'tap into natural energy?' You ever tapped into the 'natural energy' of a curse?"

Wendy pursed her full lips. "Curses are very complex. Many witches believe that they are never to be touched and others believe that they can be used, with caution, under certain extreme circumstances-"

Beth advanced, her silver cross clutched tightly in her hand like a weapon. "Answer the question. Have you ever placed a curse on anyone?"

"Sort of."

Derek and Ed drew back from her. Brandon dropped Joan's hand and stepped toward his ex. "You what?"

She sighed. "I told you, it's a complicated issue! Sometimes a curse is justified. I'm not saying yours were justified. I don't know all the details. But I know of some that were."

Derek raised a hand, fixing her in an intent stare. "When you say 'sort of,' what exactly does that mean?"

"I haven't personally put a curse on anyone. But I strengthened one that someone else did. A long time ago. My mother."

Beth gasped, taking a step backward. "You put a curse on your own mother?"

"No! My mother placed a curse. And I strengthened it. I—"

An ear-splitting scream shot into the room. The group whirled toward the doorway, all together like a startled synchronized swimming team, to find a ghostly-pale Veronica pointing a shaking finger at Wendy.

"You! Who are you? And what were you doing in my vision this morning?"

CHAPTER 13

Still in synchronicity, the team slowly swiveled to look at Wendy, who seemed just as flustered as everyone else, her eyes darting from person to person before settling on Veronica at last.

Joan stepped forward, finally dropping Brandon's hand and crossing her arms. "Well? Any idea why you appeared in her vision?"

"What vision?" Wendy's formerly sultry voice had risen an octave and she sounded like a bewildered child. "I don't know what you're talking about."

Veronica advanced, leaving the three newcomers crowding together in the doorway, confusion painted across their faces. "I meditated with the key this morning and you showed up in the visions I saw with my third eye."

Wendy froze. "Key? What key?"

Beth grabbed the box with the key from the table, and before anyone could stop her, she pulled it out and held it aloft. From the doorway, Joan heard gasps as her classmates saw the key and felt the curse resonating. There went the whole reason for them being here; there would be no point in testing them now.

Wendy didn't gasp. Her eyes narrowed and for a split second, a sly grin flashed across her face. An instant later it was gone and Joan found herself wondering if it had happened at all. Wendy held out her hand. "May I see that?"

Beth hesitated, but she handed it over, her face creased in a suspicious scowl.

Wendy turned it over in her hand, examining it closely. "Now, I was under the impression that this was some kind of support group for people who had been cursed. But now I'm getting the idea that maybe you were all cursed together?"

"Yeah," Brandon said. "I thought I told you, we were cursed when we were kids."

"I guess it slipped my mind. Your whole class, huh?"

Joan froze, her mind churning furiously. They hadn't said they were a class. And Wendy had *recognized* the key. This witch knew something. Had anyone else seen the look on her face? She needed to tell someone before they trusted her with too much information.

"Hey, Veronica," she said brightly. "Your poor dog has been cooped up in the house all morning, hasn't she? What do you say you and I take her for a quick walk in the woods?"

"Really? I thought you hated-"

Joan emitted a manic giggle, and her voice came out way too shrill. "What? I love dogs!"

She struggled to modulate her voice and ended up going an octave lower than usual. "Willow is just precious."

She cleared her throat and finally got it right. "Come on, let's go. It's getting too crowded in here anyway."

"Oh. Sure, okay. Wonderful." Joan led Veronica outside and then into the house, where Veronica collapsed on a kitchen chair, bursting into laughter.

"What is your deal?" Joan stared at her in shock.

Veronica tried to stop laughing, but every time she looked at Joan's increasingly annoyed face, she started back up again. Finally, she calmed down, wiping tears from her eyes. "Oh, I needed that. Don't quit your day job to become a spy — that was the most awkward display of nonchalance I've ever seen. But you're fantastic at code words. Never in a million years would I have suspected that the word 'precious' would pass your lips, sweetie."

"Don't call me that."

Veronica beamed at her. "So. Wendy is clearly up to something. Did you see the look on her face when Beth showed her that key?"

"You saw that too, huh? We better actually get Willow, though. She's sneaky — if she suspects us, she might be watching to see that we're really walking the dog."

Veronica nodded soberly and went into the guest room, emerging a moment later with Willow on a bright pink leash.

As they walked across the yard and toward the woods, Joan glanced at the window and saw that Wendy was indeed watching them. She focused on keeping her face pleasant, nodding enthusiastically as Veronica chattered about Willow's grain-free diet.

Finally, they reached the path that twisted through the two acres of woods at the back of Joan's property. There was a bench just inside the forest, carefully placed out of sight of the rest of the yard to create the illusion of being surrounded by wilderness. No one in the lab would be able to see them if they sat down there.

Veronica took a seat, unhooking Willow's leash to allow her to explore. "So tell me what the witch was saying before I got there. What do we know about her?"

Joan sat beside her and quickly ran through the little Brandon had told her and then the events leading up to Veronica's arrival.

When she'd finished, Veronica closed her eyes for a moment, sitting perfectly still, meditating or something. At least she didn't feel the need to get naked this time. Joan waited, glancing around the clearing. She really needed to get out here with a weedwhacker soon.

Veronica interrupted her train of thought. "Wendy is Mrs. Olsen's daughter."

Joan jumped to her feet. "What?!"

"Think about it. She didn't know that Brandon was part of a group curse, but when she found out, she said 'class,' even though no one else had said that. She clearly recognized the key. She said she strengthened a curse placed by her mother a long time ago. And when I saw her in my vision, I thought she looked like Mrs. Olsen. I still think so. I wonder why Brandon never saw it?"

"I don't think he had Mrs. Olsen on the mind when he was dating her. And she doesn't look *that* much like her."

"Do you disagree?"

"No, like you said, it's around the eyes. Yeah, now that you point all that out, it's obvious. So what are we going to do?"

"Tricky." Veronica tapped a manicured fingernail against her lips.

Joan's phone chirped and she dug it out of her back pocket. She clicked on the text from Brandon. *You better come back. Wendy's gone. Beth kicked her out.*

"Oh, crap."

"What is it?"

Joan showed Veronica the text. "Well, at least she's gone and we can talk without her overhearing."

They started back to the lab, Willow following behind. "Yes, but now we can't keep an eye on her. Who knows what she'll do with the info we just gave her."

"Maybe she'll remove the curse. Didn't you say that she's obsessed with Brandon?"

"Sure, but she hates me, and now she probably hates Beth too. And most people who interact with Derek for more than two seconds hate him. The balance is stacked against us."

Joan pushed open the door to the lab and they walked into an uncharacteristically non-argumentative conversation, leaving Willow outside in the yard.

Derek waved them in without pausing in his discourse, "Okay, but if Susan didn't react, then we need to discern what it is that she and Ed have in common. Therein may lie an answer to immunity or a cure."

Susan shrugged. "Yeah, but I mean, I didn't get hit that hard by the curse on the day of, you know?"

"Wait, Susan didn't get a jolt either?" Joan asked, taking a seat on a stool. "That's huge!"

Brandon nodded. "Paul and Lily did, though."

Veronica interjected. "I think we need to do some damage control with Wendy before we can start dealing with this new info. She has to be Mrs. Olsen's daughter, right?"

Brandon gasped, his face paling. "You've got to be kidding me!"

"Makes sense to me," Ed remarked. "Her mom probably got her into witchcraft to begin with."

"I would guess that her strengthening of the curse is what brought on Veronica and Beth's renewed symptoms," remarked Derek. "She certainly recognized the key as well; I wonder if she used it as a focus."

"How did it end up in the antique store, then?" Joan wondered.

Derek waved a hand in a gesture of dismissal. "Doesn't matter. What matters is that we find out whether what she's learned today can help her strengthen the curse further or even trigger it early."

Joan turned to Brandon. "You better go after her."

"Me? I can't do that!"

"You're the only one she might talk to!"

"She's right," agreed Veronica. "She hates the rest of us."

Brandon bit his lip. "Fine. But if she murders me, it's on you."

"Fair enough." Joan nodded. She stepped up to him and gave him a peck on the cheek. "Good luck out there. Be sure to text us if you are about to be murdered."

He rolled his eyes and pulled out his phone to call Wendy, hitting Send as he strode out of the lab. Sadie's voice drifted in from outside. "Hey, Mr. Grumpypants, what's eating you?"

There was no response, and a moment later, Sadie bounded into the room. "What's eating Mr. Grumpypants out there?"

"Oh, you know, turns out he's slept with the enemy. Or the enemy's daughter at least," Joan replied, waving her in.

"Oh, well, sure, that'd get anyone's aglets in a twist."

"Aha!" Ed pointed a triumphant finger in the air. "It is a saying!"

"But it doesn't make any sense," Joan protested.

"Why not?" Sadie asked, setting her bag of medical supplies on the card table and shrugging out of her coat, all in one smooth motion.

"Aglets are just the little plastic thingies at the end of your shoelaces. Too small to twist."

"Really?" Sadie laughed. "I always thought it had something to do with apron strings."

Sadie noticed the new arrivals and hurled herself at Susan, throwing her arms around her. "Hey! Susan, I haven't seen you in a million years! What's going on, girl?"

"Oh, you know, business as usual." As Susan responded, Sadie moved on to hug Lily as well and then gave Paul an enthusiastic high five. "The album's almost done. You gotta hit up one of our gigs one of these days."

"Where are you guys playing next?"

"Trophy Room this Friday. You free?"

Sadie nodded vigorously. "Joan and I'll be there, for sure."

Joan sighed inwardly. Susan's jam band sound wasn't really her cup of tea.

Derek rubbed his temples as he interrupted the chit chat. "Can we please focus? You're late, Sadie, and quite a lot has happened; we won't be needing your phlebotomy services after all. Perhaps someone could catch you up and then we can work on formulating a plan to move forward?"

"Well," Joan began, "in a nutshell, Brandon's ex is Mrs. Olsen's daughter, she's been strengthening the curse, possibly using the key, and she now hates us even more because Beth pissed her off."

"I didn't do anything wrong!" Beth objected. "Did you really want her hanging around here?"

Ed shook his head. "No, Beth, you're right. We wouldn't have been able to get anything done if she'd stuck around."

"But we might have kept her in a good mood," pointed out Lily. "I hope Brandon can at least distract her from going straight home and setting extra curses on us."

"We'll just have to trust Brandon to handle that as well as he can; worrying about it won't help us," said Derek. "What I would like to discuss now is the similarities between Ed and Susan."

"Why?" Sadie asked. "Are you two getting together?"

Joan sighed. "Not everything is about sex, Sadie."

She pouted. "Well, it should be! So what is it about, then? The curse, I suppose."

"We're the only two who haven't had any reaction to the key so far," Ed told her.

"No reaction? I thought everyone was getting a jolt."

"Not us," said Susan. "Everyone else. So far."

"Well, I still haven't seen it! Maybe you should test me now," Sadie suggested. "No one else has died, have they?"

"Just Beth," Joan said.

Paul lifted a hand, staring at Beth. "What do you mean 'died?' She looks fine to me."

"Beth and I both had extreme reactions," Veronica said. "We technically died for a moment and were then revived."

"And you're just casually waving that key around?" Lily was flabbergasted.

Derek clapped his hands twice for attention. "Hey! I'm not going to say it again! We need to focus!" He held up a notebook. On it, he had written the names of everyone who had seen the key, in two columns. Ed, Susan, and Wendy were in one and everyone else in the other. He pointed to the second column. "Now, here are all the people who have had reactions to the key." He indicated the other side. "And here are the ones who haven't. One of these was not cursed. The other two were." He turned to Joan. "Do you have any neighbors or anyone around who isn't cursed, who we could show the key to and see if they react? I'm not concerned about hooking them up to the machines at this point. I just want to make sure we can definitively correlate the curse and the key."

Sadie skipped to the door and called out, "Hey, Marlon! Becca! Get in here!"

Joan cocked her head. "Why aren't they in school?"

Sadie shrugged. "Becca wasn't feeling well, and I figured Marlon would probably catch it too, so why send him to school to spread it around? They can be control guinea pigs."

"But people have died. They could die," objected Lily, looking wildly around the room, gesturing toward Veronica and Beth in turn.

Becca bounced into the lab. "Die? Really? Cool."

"You're not going to die, Becca," Sadie assured her. "Beth and Veronica just died for a moment, and their circumstances were very different from yours."

"What about me?" Marlon asked, walking in more sedately.

"Nope! And I'm going to do it too, at the same time."

"Okay, cool. What do we have to do?"

Derek set up three stools in a row. "The three of you should sit down so we can all see your reactions." He gestured to Joan and Veronica. "You two get ready just in case we do need to resuscitate. Does anyone else know CPR?"

Lily raised a hand.

"Okay, you stand over here too."

Joan grabbed the defibrillator from the table and quickly readied it for use, as Veronica and Lily positioned themselves behind the stools to catch anyone if they should fall. Lily fidgeted nervously.

Derek nodded to Beth. "Do you have the key?"

She nodded and held up the box. "Ready?"

Becca gave a perky thumbs-up, and Marlon a solemn nod. Sadie grinned broadly.

Beth opened the box and held up the key.

Sadie gasped, drawing back. Veronica lept to catch her, but she recovered quickly. Becca and Marlon just aimed puzzled frowns at their mother.

"Is something supposed to happen?" Becca asked.

"No, honey, not for you," Sadie replied shakily. "We were hoping it wouldn't affect you two."

"Then why are you so pale?" Marlon hopped off his seat and put a concerned arm around Sadie's shoulders.

"I'll be okay, Marlon. Remember how I told you guys about the crazy lady who cursed me and Auntie Joan in first grade?"

They nodded, glancing at Joan, who gave them a new version of her encouraging smile. Their mystified expressions shifted into terror. She dropped the smile.

Sadie continued. "Well, this is related to that. But it's good because it means we might be able to fix it before the curse comes back. Okay?"

"Okay," they chorused.

"Now go back outside, so we can work on fixing it."

The twins ran back out into the yard.

Just then, a text came through to Joan's phone, and she pulled it out. Brandon again. *I won't be back; spending the day with Wendy. She's precious and I think we're getting back together.*

Joan frowned. "What the fuck?"

Derek spun to face her. "What now?"

"Brandon just texted me." She read them the text.

"Oh, hell no!" Sadie jumped to her feet, ready to charge out and defend her best friend's honor. "That skank is not—"

"It's obviously fake," Veronica interrupted. "He's sending us a message. Same code word you used earlier about Willow to get me to go outside with you. Brandon's in trouble."

Chapter 14

Joan's eyes widened. "We have to go after him! She must have made him text me so we wouldn't get suspicious."

Derek sighed, shaking his head. "This is like an episode of *Scooby-Doo*. Fine." He pointed to Sadie, Veronica, and Joan. "You, you, and you go rescue Brandon from the witch, who will undoubtedly turn out to be a fat man in a witch costume. The rest of us will remain here and — dare I dream it? — finally formulate a theory about the curse and the removal thereof."

Joan rushed out of the lab and back to the house to grab her purse, pulling it over her head to rest in its habitual place on her hip. Then she led Sadie and Veronica to her car and sped toward Brandon's apartment.

"I really hope she wouldn't have taken him to her house," Joan remarked. "I have no idea where she lives."

"Didn't you say she works in Salem?" Veronica asked from the back seat. "That's a good hour away; if she lives there, they wouldn't even have been able to get there yet."

"Lots of people have crazy commutes; she could live in Alexandria, Salem, or anywhere in between," Sadie pointed out. She was scrolling through a list of photos on her phone and finally clicked on one. "Here! I found her profile. Wendy Sharp. I was looking for Olsen, but I guess Brandon would have figured it out if that was her last name. Says here that she does live in Salem."

"Well, then hopefully she opted for somewhere closer," said Veronica. Her voice had an oddly strained quality to it, and Joan glanced in the mirror to see that she was holding the safety handle over the door with white knuckles, her jaw clenched and eyes squeezed shut. "Do you think we could slow down a little?"

Joan ran a red light. "Are you kidding? Who knows what that crazy witch is doing to Brandon right now?"

"Ohmigod, you guys." Sadie's voice sparkled with intensity.

"What?" As Joan careened around a corner a block away from Brandon's place, she peeked over at Sadie, who was staring at the phone in her hand, her eyes wide, mouth forming a shocked O.

"Under 'relatives.' Father: Mark Sharp. Mother: Marian Olsen. Mrs. Olsen has a profile on here too."

Joan pulled into the parking lot of Brandon's building, hurled the car into a spot, and slammed to a stop. "Let me see that." She grabbed the phone from Sadie's unresisting hands and clicked on Mrs. Olsen's picture. The profile was private, no info available, but the picture showed an older version of the teacher she remembered. And side-by-side, the resemblance to Wendy was undeniable.

Veronica leaned over the seatback to look. "But we've searched and searched for her online. Now suddenly she appears?"

"She's getting complacent," Sadie suggested. "Maybe she figured after this long, no one would be looking for her."

Joan shook her head and unbuckled her seatbelt. "Let's worry about this once we have Brandon back."

They opened their doors and jumped out of the car. Joan ran to Brandon's door, then hesitated, key in hand. "Should I open it? What if the noise tips her off?"

"It's on the first floor," Veronica said. "Let's start with the window."

They crept around the side of the building, navigating saplings, hostas, and other landscaping perils. Joan looked up at the sill. She jumped into the air, but it was too high off the ground for any of them to see in. Why couldn't it ever be easy?

"Here." Sadie cupped her hands and bent forward, offering them to Veronica. "You're tall. Put your foot here. Joan, you do the other foot, and we'll lift her up so she can see."

"Just like in cheer!" Veronica exclaimed.

"Yeah, except we weren't cheerleaders," Joan pointed out.

"I was!"

"Sadie and I weren't! We're going to drop you."

"I trust you."

Sadie, still bent with her hands cupped, twisted her neck to narrow her eyes at Joan. "Look, do you want to rescue your prince or not?"

"Fine." Joan stooped and cupped her hands, positioning them next to Sadie's. Veronica braced herself on Joan's shoulder, placed her left foot in Sadie's hands, and heaved herself up. Her other foot smacked into Joan's hands and Joan fought to keep her balance as Veronica straightened her knees and grabbed onto the window sill to steady herself.

Joan wobbled as Veronica peered into the window. She planted her legs firmly and concentrated on keeping her arms stable.

"What do you see?" Sadie hissed.

"Nothing. It's the bedroom and there's no one in here."

Sadie smirked at Joan. "Well, that's something anyway."

"I wasn't worried about that. Healthy relationships are built on trust," Joan said through gritted teeth.

"You think you and Brandon have a healthy relationship?"

Veronica looked down at them. "I have a lot of thoughts on that topic, but I don't think this is really the time!" She pointed to the next window over. "Is that one his too?"

"Yeah."

"Cool. Let's slide over."

"What do you mean 'slide over?'" Joan demanded. "You mean you're gonna stay up there?"

"Yeah, it's more efficient. Just move in tandem and take it slow. It's easy."

"Okay," Sadie nodded to Joan. "Ready? On three."

"Do what on three? I am in way over my head."

Sadie gestured toward the window with her head. "Just step to your left on three. It's not that complicated. You can do quantum physics, but not cheerleading? You're blonde and have big tits. This is what you were designed for."

"I have average-sized tits!"

Veronica sighed. "Guys, can we just move? I feel like you're over-complicating it. Just count to three and move together, and we can check the other window, okay?"

Joan took a deep breath. "Yeah. Right. On three. One. Two. Three." She took a large step to the left and smacked into Sadie.

Veronica gave a little shriek as Joan threw her elbow at the brick wall in front of her to steady herself, regaining her balance.

"What the hell, Sadie? Why didn't you move?" Joan demanded.

"I did move! I thought we were moving slowly. You took a huge step!"

"It seemed more efficient to take fewer steps! That means large ones!"

"We should have talked about that!"

"Guys!" Veronica interrupted. "With the way you're shouting at each other, we might as well have just unlocked the damn door!"

"Sorry," muttered Joan. "Should we step again?"

"On three," Sadie said. "One. Two. Three."

This time, Joan took a smaller step and Veronica shrieked again as her legs splayed. Joan hastily took another step to catch up with Sadie. "What, now we're taking big steps suddenly?"

"I thought that's what we were doing!"

"Well, I thought we were taking small ones!"

"It doesn't matter," said Veronica. "I'm at the window now." She peered in. "And I don't see anything. It's the kitchen and it looks like there's an open floor plan? I can't see the other side of the room, but there's no lights on. I don't think they're here."

"Well, crap," Joan pursed her lips. "What do we do now?"

"Put me down."

"Okay, what do we do?"

"Just put me down."

"We've never done this before," Sadie said.

"Well, I've always been the flyer. I don't know how you put someone down. There's no room here for a flip, and besides, I'm thirty-five!"

"Okay, okay," said Joan. "On three, let's just lower our hands."

"Right. Sure. On three. One. Two. Three."

Joan began to stoop, bringing her hands down, then realized that Sadie was lowering hers much faster. She adjusted her speed, but it was too late. With one more shriek, Veronica tumbled sideways directly on top of Joan's head and the two of them pitched over into the thick mulch, knocking loose a cloud of pungent dust, Veronica landing in a straddle across Joan's waist.

Sadie rushed to help Veronica up. "Are you guys okay?"

"I think so." Joan hauled herself to her feet, checking for any injuries or soreness. "Yeah, I'm good."

"Me too," said Veronica, brushing herself off. "So where do we check next?"

"Bar?" suggested Sadie.

"Yeah." They hurried back to the car and Joan threw it in reverse, as Veronica resumed her crash position. But the bar was just a few minutes away and they arrived without incident, even finding a parking spot right in front. Joan spotted Brandon's Honda parked nearby and pointed it out.

"Great! So what's the plan, then?" Veronica asked.

"Find Brandon," said Joan.

"Well, we seem to have done that. What comes after find?"

"Rescue Brandon," Sadie said.

"How?"

"Let's just go in and see if he needs rescuing! Maybe he's already rescued himself."

Joan shook her head. "He would have texted me if he wasn't in danger anymore. He had to know we'd crack his code and come after him."

"Okay, so we're just going to barge in there?" Veronica asked. "What if that puts him in further jeopardy?"

"Do you have any actual suggestions or do you just take joy in poking holes in our plans?" Joan demanded.

"I guess not."

"Fine. Let's go." They approached the door and Sadie opened it a crack, peeking into the bar.

"What do you see?" Veronica asked. "Are they in there?"

She twisted her head around. "No one's in there."

"No one?"

"It's 9:30 in the morning. Of course no one's in there."

"Why are they even open this early?" Veronica asked.

"There's probably a few people back in the lotto room," Sadie said. "Those gamblers are crazy. I don't get it personally; I mean, if you're going to waste—"

"Who's working?" interrupted Joan.

Sadie peered in again. "Alison. I think I'm freaking her out." She dropped the door handle, letting the door fall closed.

"Well, let's go ask if she's seen him." Joan nudged Sadie aside and opened the door wide, striding into the bar and navigating the path between the tables. The perky bartender gave her a big, sunny smile.

"Hi, Joan! Was that you peeking in a second ago?"

She gestured behind her. "That was Sadie. You know Sadie — she's a weirdo. This is Veronica. Have you seen Brandon?"

"Oh, um." Alison twisted her long magenta braid between two fingers and nervously glanced toward the door to the basement. "I don't know how to tell you this, but he went downstairs about twenty minutes ago with an extreme babe who seemed super into him."

"Yeah," said Sadie. "And we're here to kick her ass. May we?" She gestured toward the door.

"I don't know..." Alison hesitated.

"Come on," Joan wheedled. "I've been down there dozens of times with Brandon. It's not like we're just random passersby. Sadie and I are your best customers!"

"Yeah, all right. But don't tell Jessica."

"Never," Sadie promised.

They rushed for the basement door and Joan punched in four numbers. "See? I already know the code."

They pulled the door open and tiptoed onto the stairs, Veronica closing it lightly behind them. Joan put a finger to her lips and the trio tiptoed down the stairs.

They were almost to the bottom when Brandon's voice drifted up to them. Joan put her arm out to hold the others back.

"You know that if you do this, I'll never bone you again, right?"

Sadie put her lips next to Joan's ear. "He'd better never bone her again regardless."

She choked back a laugh, gesturing wildly for Sadie to shut the hell up. Veronica nudged her and nodded her head toward the right, where the light was coming from. They crept down the last couple of stairs and Joan cautiously peered around the wall in the relevant direction.

The light emanated from the open door of the manager's office, about twelve feet away, beyond a couple of pallets of liquor cases. Joan stepped out of the shelter of the staircase and into the storeroom. Sadie and Veronica followed, the three of them sneaking toward the doorway.

They heard no response from Wendy, but Brandon wasn't finished. "Why do you care so much about this curse anyway? How is your life improved by me and a bunch of strangers going blind and dumb?"

As she got closer, Joan could hear movement from the room, but Wendy still wasn't talking. She was no Bond villain, apparently.

Joan wrinkled her nose. Why did it smell like weed in here? If anyone had been smoking on their break, the manager was going to flip out. Jessica had a strict policy about drinking or drugs during shifts.

Brandon tried one more time. "How come you weren't in our class, if Mrs. Olsen was your mom? You're the same age as me, right?"

Joan flattened herself against the wall next to the entrance and carefully poked her head around the doorframe, taking in as many details as she could before ducking back out. Brandon was seated on a wooden chair in the middle of the room, his back to the door and his hands zip-tied behind him. The chair sat smack in the middle of a pentagram drawn with some dark green substance sprinkled on the floor.

Wendy stood off to the side, staring intently at a tablet in her hands, even though every instinct told Joan that it should have been a huge leatherbound book chained to a podium. The witch finally answered Brandon, speaking slowly, dreamily, almost absentmindedly. "I was raised by my dad. I never met my mom until a couple years ago."

"Really? So she abandoned you, huh?"

Joan tensed as she heard a slapping sound. She peeked back into the room to see Wendy standing over Brandon, her hand raised as though to hit him again. Sadie, who knew Joan well, grabbed her arm and hauled her back before she could rush in and tackle Wendy.

Veronica glided silently toward a corner of the storeroom and gestured to the others to join her. Joan reluctantly complied, allowing Sadie to pull her by the hand, but walking backward to keep an eye on the gaping doorway. As Sadie and Veronica began to whisper, she finally turned and began to pay attention.

"She's obviously planning to use him for some kind of ritual. Did you see that pentagram?" murmured Veronica. "We have to stop her and get Brandon out of there. I have a plan." She outlined it for them quickly.

It was completely insane. But it was the best they had.

CHAPTER 15

Joan finished placing the last of the supply shelves and stepped back to survey their work. It had taken half an hour and a crapload of WD-40 on the casters to silently inch them into place.

She wiped her sweaty palms on her jeans and took a shaky breath in. She jumped, startled, as Veronica crept up behind her and touched her shoulder.

"Don't do that!" she hissed.

"Are you sure these are all in the right spots?" Veronica whispered.

"Yeah, it's pretty basic physics, actually. Do you remember the order to push them over?"

Veronica nodded, but her face was anything but sure. "I think so."

"Let's just run through them again," Joan suggested.

"Thanks."

"Sure — so I'll start with that one." She pointed. "The noise from it will draw her out. Right? Then which one will you push?"

Veronica hesitated, then leveled a finger toward another shelf. "That one, right? Toward the door?"

Joan nodded. "Right. And then I push . . . ?"

Veronica pointed again. "That one. And then I do that one over there. And then you do that one. And then I push that one—"

"Nope. That's the last one."

"Right. This one here." Veronica poked a carton of straws on the shelf directly in front of them. "And then that one is last."

"Yeah. One more time."

Veronica ran through it again, correctly this time. Satisfied, Joan got into position at her first shelf, waiting for Veronica to do the same. Then she pulled out her phone and texted Sadie. *We're ready. Make the call.*

The plan would work best if Brandon knew they were rescuing him, so Sadie had gone upstairs to place a call from her cell to the bar. She would instruct Alison not to answer, and after a few rings, it would go to the answering machine in the office. She would leave a message full of coded hints for Brandon to hear, letting him know something was up.

The phone rang. Joan strained her ears to hear what was happening in the office but could only hear the *BRRRRRRRRRRRRRRRIIIIIING* of a landline phone. She lifted a hand, holding up one finger.

It rang again and she unfolded a second finger.

Third ring. Third finger. She pointed at the door. The machine always clicked on after three rings.

The ringing stopped, but the machine didn't click on. Joan frowned into the silence. She sidled toward the office door.

She stopped just outside the doorway and peered in. Wendy was seated at the desk, looking at her tablet again, scrolling down a page, frowning in concentration. There was an empty, slightly discolored space in the corner of the desktop where the old beat-up black answering machine used to sit. Where was it?

Joan desperately searched the office, eyes roving everywhere, to no avail. Suddenly she spotted it, in the worst possible location – crammed into the wastebasket, its spiral cord wrapped around its slim rectangular body.

And then, into the hush, her cell phone went *CHIRP.*

Joan ducked away from the door, just as Wendy's head was snapping up.

She sprinted toward the safety of the shelves, calling out in the loudest quiet voice she could muster, "Start it! Push over the first shelf!"

She skidded to a halt behind the shelter of a rack of beer bottles as the first shelving unit came crashing down and pulled her phone out to see what urgent missive had so derailed their plan. Sadie. *No more machine! The call forwarded to Jessica's cell!*

Great. Everything derailed because she forgot to silence her phone and Sadie felt the need to communicate the obvious. She glanced up and saw Wendy silhouetted in the doorway, motionless, calmly examining the carnage of shelf number one, watching the room for motion.

Joan looked around herself and found that she had instinctively run to the correct spot; she was in position to push down the second shelf. But Wendy wasn't where she was supposed to be – they had planned on her heading behind the first rack to see what had happened. Then they would push them down in order to trap her within.

There was no point in pushing down the second shelf. Unless maybe that would draw her out. But it couldn't be the order they planned, because then Wendy wouldn't have the right path into the middle of the circle....

Joan studied the arrangement, sorting the shelves and the angles in her mind. The one that Veronica would have done third would be perfect; just skip the second one, draw Wendy over there, and then proceed as planned.

She locked eyes with Veronica, who was staring at her with bleak desperation on her face. She held up three fingers and made a *pushing* gesture. Veronica furrowed her brow, her eyes darting back and forth, looking for a clue to what the gesture meant. Joan pointed to the shelf in question and mimed pushing it again.

Veronica's face brightened and she tiptoed to the correct spot, glancing up at Joan again for confirmation. Joan nodded emphatically.

Veronica pulled the shelf and it thundered to the floor, smashing glasses and battering the concrete floor with its metal supports. Joan spun around to gauge Wendy's reaction.

The witch remained still, moving only her head to peer in this new direction. Her eyes narrowed.

Joan and Veronica remained frozen in place, watching Wendy.

Slowly, Wendy took a step into the storeroom. She stopped, moving her head this way and that, gazing into the dim room. She turned around and Joan saw her look toward the doorway, spotting the light switch.

Thank goodness they'd thought of that. Wendy flipped the switch, but Veronica had removed the bulbs before they'd started rearranging everything.

Wendy growled in frustration. She turned back to look at the shelves again, a frown marring her beautiful face. Good. People who were angry made mistakes.

Joan ignored the little voice in her head that pointed out that she was also angry. That was different. She had right on her side. She turned back to Veronica and pointed to each of the racks in turn, indicating to return to the original order. Veronica gave her a thumbs up and moved silently to her next position.

Wendy glided forward into the midst of the shelves and Joan braced herself, waiting until she was in the right spot. Then she gave a mighty shove and the shelf crashed down. This one was filled with napkins, so it was less dramatic and a little disappointing. She shrugged and moved toward her next position.

Joan froze as Wendy began to mutter to herself. Her eyes widened, staring at Wendy's hands, which had begun to glow.

Chapter 16

Joan looked at Veronica again, only to find her completely checked out, her eyes closed, hands folded on her heart. Great. What a fabulous time for a meditation break.

She turned her focus back to Wendy, nervously watching the golden orb of light developing between her outstretched palms, the first active magic she'd seen since Mrs. Olsen had cursed them. Maybe Brandon was right — this didn't look like garden-variety Wicca.

She bit her lip, thinking furiously.

Should they continue their plan? It was Veronica's turn, though, and there was no way to get across the circle they'd been making to heave the shelf over herself. She silently jumped up and down a couple of times, waving to get Veronica's attention, but the other woman's eyes remained closed.

Joan was on her own, for the moment, anyway. She could push over a different rack and hope Veronica would get the message to keep going. It was tough to know what to do without knowing what that ball of magic was for. And without knowing what the hell Veronica was doing.

She glanced at Wendy's hands again. The orb was growing tendrils, which were traveling in several directions, branching off from the main light. It had a creepy vibe, as though it was *searching* for something. Or someone.

Joan snuck a peek at Wendy's face, which was closed down — completely blank. Eyes closed, mouth slack, cheeks and brows relaxed. Like the light was taking all of her consciousness. And the tendrils were starting to gather in the opposite direction from Joan. They were, in fact, creeping directly toward Veronica, who had moved into some kind of yoga warrior pose, her stance wide, her arms straight, palms facing out toward Wendy.

Making a snap decision, Joan moved toward the office, keeping her eyes on Wendy. This proved to be a mistake, as she immediately banged her shin on the fallen napkin rack.

Joan clenched her fists, her face, and her feet all at once to keep from screaming and cursing. Why the shin? The only thing worse was stubbing your toe.

She opened her eyes cautiously and saw with relief that Wendy didn't appear to have heard anything.

She kept moving, making her way carefully around the prone shelving units. When she finally reached the office door, she risked another glance over her shoulder. A branch of energy was just a couple of inches from Veronica's palm.

Joan hesitated. Maybe she should go back. She watched as the probe reached her friend's hand... and was gently rebuffed. The energy simply drifted past, with no reaction from either Veronica or Wendy.

Joan raised her eyebrows. Maybe Veronica really was a guru. She shrugged and turned to enter the office — and stubbed her toe on the doorframe.

Her head snapped backward and her lips parted in a silent howl to the heavens. She grabbed the doorknob for support, hopping on one foot into the room.

She stopped just short of the pentagram. Up close, she could see that it was formed from some kind of crumpled herb —

something mystical, rare, and powerful, no doubt, grown in a sacred grove and harvested in the dark of the moon.

Brandon was still seated in the center of it, his head hanging as though he was asleep — or unconscious. Or dead. No. He couldn't be dead.

She felt completely out of her element, with no idea whether this spell followed the parameters of the witchcraft she thought she knew. Would it be safe to enter the pentagram? Pop culture was pretty mixed on that point, and that's all she really had to go on, besides cryptic references from dusty old tomes about time-based magic and inherited elemental powers.

Tentatively, Joan poked a finger into the space above the line. Then a little bit past it. Nothing happened. She stepped inside and waited, breath bated, eyes scrunched closed. Nothing happened and she opened one eye and then the other. The room seemed to be the same as it had been before.

She circled around Brandon's chair until she was directly in front of him and then reached for his neck. She released a grateful sigh as she felt his pulse jump beneath her fingers, and she pulled him into her arms, fighting back tears. He was alive.

"Joan? Holy fuck, babe, I have never been so glad to see anyone in my whole fucking life." Brandon's whisper pulled her back to reality.

"We gotta get you out of here," she said. "Veronica's handling Wendy, I guess."

"You guess?"

She shrugged. "Our plan didn't go as... planned. We were supposed to be trapping Wendy in a pyramid of fallen shelves and then Sadie was going to call the cops, but—" Joan stood up and circled back around to Brandon's hands to cut off his ties. "Oh, crap."

"What?"

"We were going to use Veronica's knife to get these ties off."

"Wait, Veronica carries a knife?"

"I know, right? Surprised the crap out of me. One of those utility knives you clip to a belt. She keeps it in the inside pocket of her yoga pants."

"She has pockets in her yoga pants?"

"It's a whole lifestyle thing; fancy yoga pants with pockets. How the hell are we going to get these off?"

He nodded toward the purse at her hip. "You got anything in your bag?"

She thrust her hand deep into the main compartment, rummaging blindly, shoving aside pens, wallet, loose change, keys — her hand froze. Was it...? Could it be...?

She gripped a small oblong object and pulled it out. It was! Her corkscrew! The good one with the foil cutter on the side! She took a moment to do a teeny tiny happy dance in place before getting down to business.

Joan knelt beside Brandon once again and unfolded the tiny blade on the side. She sawed at the zip ties, and little by little they came apart.

"Got it!" She pulled the ties off of him, waving them triumphantly over her head.

Brandon jumped to his feet, rubbing his wrists. "Okay, let's get Veronica and get out of here."

She folded up the corkscrew, stowing it back in her purse and then stood and grabbed his hand.

They crept to the door and peered out into the storeroom.

Veronica was lit up like a Grateful Dead concert. Beams of mystical light surrounded her on all sides but were completely ignoring her.

Wendy remained motionless, eyes still closed, apparently trusting her spell to find anyone around. If she'd just opened her eyes, she definitely would have seen her prey immediately.

Joan fought the urge to snicker. Instead, she led Brandon carefully around all of their obstacles, pointing silently to two of the shelves, miming to him the order in which to push them. Then she took up position beside Veronica to take over her half.

She held up a finger, then two, then three and then pointed to Brandon. He pushed over a rack and she immediately followed suit. He pushed his and she pushed hers, and within a second, Wendy was surrounded by shelves.

Wendy's eyes snapped open and she emitted a rage-filled shriek, dropping her hands, her spell swiftly draining backward into her palms.

Veronica dropped her warrior pose and opened her own eyes. "Got him? Let's go!"

The three of them raced up the stairs and Joan twisted the knob, heaving the door open and slamming it into the side of the stainless steel dishwasher next to it. They poured out into the bar to find several of the morning regulars staring at them.

Sadie jumped to her feet and joined them in their speedy exodus out onto the sidewalk.

As they'd planned, Sadie and Veronica raced to Joan's car. Joan dragged Brandon to his car, sliding into the passenger seat and putting on her seat belt.

Brandon revved the engine on and shifted into reverse. He turned his head, bracing his hand on the shoulder of Joan's seat and took his foot off the brake.

And then, for the third time in her life, Joan felt a jolt of electricity surge through her body.

Everything went blurry.

She lurched against the seat belt as they smacked into the car behind them with a sickening crunch.

CHAPTER 17

Joan opened her mouth to scream, but no voice emerged. Panic rose and so did bile. She hastily opened the car door and leaned out as the acidic remains of her delightful breakfast forced themselves up and out through her mouth. She finished vomiting and gagged soundlessly, trying to cough, squinting as she groped in the center console for the bottle of water Brandon always kept there. She found it with her hand and untwisted the lid, pouring the lukewarm liquid down her throat.

Her vision cleared slightly and she found herself able to make out the shape of Brandon, hunched in his seat, his head in his hands.

She touched his shoulder and he turned in her direction. She unbuckled herself and scooted closer, to the very edge of her seat, putting her head right next to his, and could hear, very faintly, his whisper. She turned so her ear was next to his lips.

"She used my blood. She had a finger stick and she took my blood. Can you hear me, Joan? She triggered the curse early."

Joan took Brandon's hand and placed it on her cheek, nodding her head to show that she understood. Then she jerked her head back toward her own car. Hopefully Sadie hadn't had time to drive off and was still there. Joan scooted out, careful to step widely out of the vehicle to avoid her mess.

Successful, she squinted again, heading for where her car was parked, but her vision had faded once more and she felt like she was in a snowstorm.

Instinctively, she tried to call out for Sadie, but of course she could make no sound.

She took a few faltering steps in what she hoped was the right direction, and then she heard her name called in a stage whisper. She followed it and ran directly into Sadie. Of course; Sadie had been able to whisper in the original curse, and her vision had only gone slightly myopic.

"Are you okay? How is Brandon?" Sadie asked.

Joan tried to answer, then shook her head and mimed instead, pointing to herself and holding her hand out parallel to the ground. She rocked it back and forth to indicate that she was okay, but not great. Then she pointed back toward Brandon and gave a thumb's down.

She heard another whisper. "How many fingers?"

Her vision cleared slightly and she saw that Sadie was holding up three fingers. Joan mimicked the gesture, and Sadie gave her a thumbs up and turned to go and see to Brandon.

Joan made her way carefully through the fuzzy air to her own car and opened the passenger seat to check on Veronica.

As she'd feared, Veronica had passed out. She felt for a pulse and found it strong, so she simply arranged her friend's limbs into a comfortable position and then sat down on the curb, holding Veronica's hand and waiting for her to wake up.

She fought down anxiety as her sight shifted frequently between blizzardlike conditions to just staticky TV, holding tightly to Veronica like a lifeline.

Finally, she felt a tug as Veronica woke up. She remembered how terrified Veronica had been during her testing when the curse had triggered for a minute. Joan stroked her hand in what she hoped was a soothing way and felt her relax slightly.

A groping hand smacked into the side of her head and she grabbed it, pulling it around to her face, allowing Veronica to feel her features to identify her.

The snowstorm lifted and she could make out Veronica's shape now. She tried to whisper to her and slumped when she couldn't. She remembered being able to whisper occasionally when she was six. Why couldn't she say anything now? Maybe it would come and go, like her sight.

Joan's heart filled with pity as she watched Veronica struggle to see and speak. She shuddered to recall Veronica's description of her complete blindness — like your eyes are closed and there are no lights on.

Sadie returned, leading Brandon, and Joan stood to allow Sadie to take her place, so she could whisper comforting words to Veronica.

As she found herself seeing nothing but white once again, Brandon's arms encircled her in pure comforting warmth. She wrapped her own arms around his waist to give what solace she could, leaning her cheek against his chest, his flannel shirt soft against her face.

As she stood there, her panic receded and her mind sharpened. She found herself thinking of the ritual Wendy performed to retrigger the curse. She must have been almost done with it when they'd interrupted; she hadn't had much time between their departure and their collapse. Maybe all she'd had to do was speak the magic words.

What had she seen in the office? Brandon in the center of the pentagram. Dried green leaves. What could that have been? Some kind of herb, maybe? She inhaled deeply, Brandon's scent soothing her. But there was another smell on him. She'd smelled it when they'd come in. An aroma she'd never smelled there before, because Jessica was so strict about it.

Cannabis. And Ed was immune to the curse now. So was Susan. What did they have in common? They were both stoners.

Joan pulled away from Brandon and tried to find Sadie. She hopped around, flailing her arms until someone grabbed her. She put her face very close to theirs, saw that it was Sadie, and waved at her urgently.

"What is it?" Sadie whispered.

Joan lifted her hand to her lips, her fingers and thumb together, and inhaled deeply in the universal sign for *smoking weed*.

Sadie stared at her. "You want to get high? Now?"

Joan sighed. How to get it across that this was the answer. She mimed playing a guitar to indicate Susan. What would represent Ed? How do you mime ghost hunting? The only thing she could think of to mimic Ed was to smoke pot, but she'd done that. She tried shading her eyes and looking around and then shivering as though she'd seen a ghost.

Sadie just shook her head. "Smoking weed, playing guitar, looking for something, cold? I feel like I'm talking to Lassie."

Just then, Brandon got it. His face lit up and he jumped up and down too. He mimed smoking a joint, just as Joan had. Joan pointed to Brandon in triumph. Sadie looked more perplexed. "You want to smoke too?"

Frustrated, Joan slumped, thinking furiously. Did it really matter if Sadie got it? As long as she just thought they wanted to get high, maybe she'd go and buy them a joint. If they smoked, maybe it would lift the curse. Whether Sadie knew that's what they were doing was irrelevant.

Joan pulled a twenty out of her pocket and handed it to Sadie. She smoked her pretend joint again and then pointed up the street, where she knew there was a dispensary.

"Seriously? You want me to go over there and buy you some pot? Right now?"

Joan nodded emphatically. Her sight was going blank again, but she hoped Brandon was reinforcing the message.

"Fine," Sadie whispered. "I'll be back soon."

Relieved, Joan grabbed Brandon's hand and squeezed tight. Then she thought about Veronica, sitting alone in the car, and pulled Brandon in that general direction. Her searching hand found the open car door and she followed its shape until she reached empty air. She gently waved her hand back and forth across the opening, finally hitting soft, yielding flesh. Oops.

Joan removed her hand from Veronica's breast, following her arm down to the hand. She clasped Veronica's hand in her left, Brandon's in her right, and settled in to wait.

As Joan sat cross-legged on the sidewalk, her mind began to drift. She closed her eyes to give her shifting sight a break. She focused on breathing evenly.

In and out. In and out.

Her body felt like it was expanding, her limbs filling with air, and her self floating off into the wind. Time stood still.

It could have been an hour or a minute. Okay, well, Sadie told her later that it was about fifteen minutes. But Joan couldn't tell; she felt so calm.

When Sadie returned, Joan felt Brandon stand up and she simply flowed upward into a standing position. According to Sadie, it looked super awkward. But Joan couldn't tell; she felt so graceful.

She dropped Brandon's hand and smiled serenely — Sadie said it was creepy, like the smile of a Victorian doll – at everything around her.

Her eyes remained closed as, without missing a beat, she walked straight to the back door of the car, her hand going straight to the handle, and opened it up. She slid in, moving all the way to the other side to make room for Brandon.

She listened as Sadie got into the driver's seat, clicked open the plastic tube containing the joint, and flicked the lighter a couple of times. She listened to the hiss of Sadie's inhale. Breathed in the sweet smoke as it filled the air in the car. Heard Sadie say — not whisper, "You want some, Veron— Holy crap! I can talk! And see! Clearly! Take a hit — I think the weed's making the curse go away!"

She heard another inhale, and Veronica whispered, "It's fuzzy, but I can see a little. Can you hear me? I can hear me a little!" Veronica coughed and Joan heard the faint sound of a water bottle unscrewing. She listened as Veronica glugged and her coughing subsided.

Joan felt Sadie's long-nailed hand grab hers and gently wrap her fingers around the joint. She held it to her lips and breathed in, forcing the harsh smoke past her raw throat, filling her lungs with it, and holding it in for a long moment. She exhaled with a *WHOOOSH.*

Her sight was still a little blurry, but much clearer. She opened her mouth and tentatively spoke. "Can I talk?"

She could talk!

"I can talk!"

Joan handed the doobie to Brandon. As they passed it around, each of them getting a little better with each hit, the car filled up like an Amsterdam coffee shop.

Sadie, the least cursed of the group, had recovered fully from just one toke. Brandon needed two, and Joan took several. If she was being totally honest, she smoked a little more than she needed to; it'd been a stressful couple of days. Finally, as Veronica smoked the dregs of it, she declared herself back to health as well.

Joan glanced out the window and saw two police officers entering the bar. "Hey, the cops are here; did you call them, Sadie?"

"Oh, yeah. Should we go in and see what happens?"

"Let's roll down the windows and let it air out in here first," Brandon said. "I know pot's legal now, but I still feel weird about hotboxing in front of cops."

They rolled down the windows and sat for a minute, each lost in their own thoughts.

Veronica broke the silence. "What about the others? Has anyone heard from Ed?"

Joan pulled her phone out of her pocket and found four missed calls and several texts. "Crap. We need to let them know about the cure. And track down everyone else in the class."

Brandon shook his head, "That's going to take forever. We can't even use texts, because how would they read them? Let's just send one person into the bar to check out that situation and the rest of us'll start making calls."

Joan opened her door. "I'll go."

"Oh, hey!" Brandon reached over the seat and grabbed her hand before she could get any further. "Get some jalapeno poppers while you're in there."

"Ooooh, and a basket of garlic fries," ordered Sadie.

"And mozzarella sticks!" said Veronica. The group turned and stared at her.

"Since when do you eat mozzarella sticks?" Sadie demanded.

"She has the munchies," Joan snickered. "Anything else I should get? I'm going for some potato skins too, for sure."

"Just get lots," said Veronica.

Epilogue

Joan nodded and banged the car door closed, heading toward the red-bricked building. As she pulled open the heavy door to the bar, she saw the two police officers heading down the basement steps. Alison, about to follow them, waved to Joan and lifted a finger to indicate she'd be right back.

Giving Alison a thumbs up, Joan wandered to her usual stool and hopped on, almost missing the seat. She giggled and waved to the cluster of customers at the other end of the bar, who were buzzing in speculation. She gave them version three of her reassuring smile and they hurriedly looked away.

"Be cool, man," she muttered to herself. "Just get the news, get the food, and get out."

The basement door slammed open and Alison charged through it. "Dude, what the hell happened down there?"

"Shhhhhhh," Joan shushed her, giggling again. "Don't tell the cops I was there, okay?"

"Okay, but will you tell me? Also, are you high?"

"It's medicinal."

"Hey, no judgment, but it just adds a little bit more weirdness to this whole bizarre situation. What's going on? I'll play along, but I feel like I deserve to know what it is I'm playing along with."

Joan got serious. "You know the curse?"

"Sure, you and Brandon are obsessed with it, and Sadie is always bitching about how you guys should get over it and move on with your lives."

Joan grinned, lifting her arms in triumph. "Now we can! The curse is over!"

Alison gave a low whistle. "So you guys really were cursed?"

"Yeah. You know that chick Brandon was with?"

"The hot one."

"She was a witch and her mom was the one who cursed us."

"Her mom was your teacher? Did Brandon know that?"

Joan shook her head and then couldn't get it to stop. She put her hands on her head, holding it still. "No, I figured it out. Well, me and Veronica. But then she kidnapped him and I saved him, because feminism, but then she triggered the curse somehow, even though we trapped her—"

"You trapped her? Where?"

Joan pointed to the basement door. "Among the shelves."

"Um. I hate to break it to you, but she's not down there," Alison said.

"What? She's gone?"

Alison shrugged. "Yeah. I went down there after you guys ran out of here, to see what had happened. The place is a mess; Jessica is going to be pissed. But there wasn't anyone there."

A chill went through Joan and she felt suddenly and completely sober. "Son of a bitch. The witch got away."

She jumped to her feet. "Cancel that food order. I gotta go!"

As she ran out of the bar, she heard Alison call after her, "But you didn't order any food!"

Author's Note:

Hiya! You've reached the end of Book 1 of the *Rhymes With Witch* series, and I'm so glad you joined this particular brand of magical chaos.

Want to keep the shenanigans going?

You can grab Book 2 right here:

If you're in the mood for something with slightly higher stakes (but still plenty of humor), you might enjoy the Mathilda Holiday series. It follows two sisters who find themselves targeted by an ancient secret society.

Start with Book 1 here:

If you're ready for something darker and more intense, try Warrior Mage Librarians — a high-stakes fantasy series about a soft-hearted scholar and a battle-hardened warrior nun who find themselves at the center of a global cryptid war.

Start with Blood Falls here:

Acknowledgements

Credit for this book must lie squarely on the shoulders of the small group of people who meet twice-weekly at a coffee shop to write and discuss our writings. If not for them, I probably wouldn't have started the book and I certainly wouldn't have finished it. Also, the baristas who kept me supplied with iced white tea (with sweetener, light on the ice) as I wrote.

Lastly, the tumblr entitled "Writing Prompts That Don't Suck," which I stumbled across in an online search for "interesting writing prompts." There I read a prompt that mentioned a skeleton key in some context or other, from which this entire book emerged.

About the Author

Anna McCluskey is an Oregon-based, semi-nomadic, almost-entirely-feral fantasy author.

Anna is the author of the *Mathilda Holiday* series, the *Rhymes With Witch* series, the *Warrior Mage Librarians* series, and the upcoming stand-alone anthology *The Bloody Unicorn and Other Delightfully Dark Drinks*.

She has had several poems published in journals and anthologies, and her short fiction has been read by at least a dozen people, many of whom murmured appreciatively about it.

For information on upcoming projects and general merriment, check out her website, www.annamccluskey.com.

9 781734 948509